The *Moby-Dick* Blues

The *Moby-Dick* Blues

Michael Strelow

[signed] Michael Strelow

For Pepe Jones
Hope you find my characters and
story engaging
Best
MS

ROUNDFIRE
BOOKS

Winchester, UK
Washington, USA

First published by Roundfire Books, 2018
Roundfire Books is an imprint of John Hunt Publishing Ltd., Laurel House, Station Approach,
Alresford, Hants, SO24 9JH, UK
office1@jhpbooks.net
www.johnhuntpublishing.com
www.roundfire-books.com

For distributor details and how to order please visit the 'Ordering' section on our website.

Text copyright: Michael Strelow 2017

ISBN: 978 1 78535 701 5
978 1 78535 702 2 (ebook)
Library of Congress Control Number: 2017934608

A CIP catalogue record for this book is available from the British Library.

Design: Stuart Davies

Printed and bound by CPI Group (UK) Ltd, Croydon, CR0 4YY, UK

We operate a distinctive and ethical publishing philosophy in
all areas of our business, from our global network of authors to
production and worldwide distribution.

For my family—believers, singers, storytellers
and the best of folk.

Arvin

I think our house was built in 1873 or 1874. My mother sometimes gives one year and sometimes the other. In the basement, the beams measure twelve inches by twelve inches for the uprights, and the floor joists are two by eight inches. I measured both and wrote the results down in a small notebook that Salome gave me for my tenth birthday. I once tried to pound a nail into a beam because I wanted to hang up my notebook in a safe place where neither Ben or Carl could find it because either one would just take it if he could. Every nail I tried to pound into the support beam bent, and it didn't matter if I pounded small or big nails. They bent right in the middle like I was trying to pound into cement. I asked Carl later why you couldn't nail anything into the beams, and he said it was because the wood was old and dry. I had a right angle used by carpenters and Carl told me he would give me twenty-five cents for every right angle—it had to be exact—I could find in the house. I couldn't find any.

Our house has had Kraft family in it every year of its life. My great-grandfather, Arvin Condon Kraft—I was named after him—cut some of the trees they made into the house. He didn't work as a carpenter or tree cutter either since he made lots of money, they said, selling his farmland to be made into new city lots. But he wanted to cut some of the oak and maple and pine trees that were going into his new house, just because. I understand that. It would be fine to point out some of the wood and say, "I cut that" or "I remember that tree when it was standing on the hillside out near Parker's Ferry."

The house has six pocket doors and five fireplaces, though all the fireplaces don't work. Three of them were plugged with metal things so we wouldn't try to start a fire, especially Ben and Carl, who like fires. I was not allowed any kind of fires in the house or out after that one time. Ben and Carl could only start fires if

1

someone—meaning mother or Salome—asked them. Our father had been dead as long as I could remember, but Ben said he could remember him and that he smelled like tobacco smoke. No one else ever smoked in our family after he was gone. Once Carl tried to get me to try to smoke a cigarette, but just the smell of it made me sick. No thanks, Carl, I told him. The pocket doors all worked in different ways. On some of them the right one stuck and the left one slid easily. Some the other way around. The doorway upstairs on the third floor, the one that closed off the highest fireplace room, sometimes the right door wouldn't budge like someone was holding it from inside the wall. Ben told me our house had ghosts and that one of them kept that door from opening when he felt like being bad and that I should never force the door. Just leave it alone when Great Uncle Morgan Kraft was feeling like holding it. Ben always told me stuff to scare me since he was older than Carl and could get away with it. Carl tried it and I'd cry because I knew he was picking on me and had been told over and over by Salome not to. Carl was afraid of Salome. Ben, too, but not as much. Salome told them both not to pick on me because I was slower than they were. Of course I was slower, I remember thinking, I'm three years younger than Carl and five years younger than Ben. I'd always be slower until we all grew up. Then I'd catch up.

The pocket doors got me thinking about the inside of the house. I shined a flashlight into the pockets to see if I could catch Great Uncle Morgan holding the door, but all I could see was way back into the wall—the dust, the track for the door, the way the plaster oozed out like frosting between the lath, and then more dark. I began to wonder if there wasn't a way to get inside the walls and see all what was in there.

A long time ago there had been servants' quarters in the basement with stairways to the outside and a big dumbwaiter as well as smaller dumbwaiters to serve each fireplace with wood. Ben explained that the house had been built to have two insides: one where people moved room to room in living spaces and the other a kind of funhouse of pulleys and hollow spaces to take things to those living spaces. Mother and Salome had forbidden us from riding on the dumbwaiters. Salome sat us down and drew us pictures (I'm sure the picture part was for me) of how the ropes could be rotten and we could fall down from the third floor and die in a bloody heap on the floor of the basement and not be found until we began to stink and rot three days later. We all said we understood, and Salome checked each one of us by looking us in the eye and then rapping us on the head with the middle knuckle of her hand to make sure we had got the message. It hurt. I hated it every time she did it, mainly to me. She said she did it because she loved me and wanted to make sure I understood what was safe and what was not safe. "I do it out of love," she always said. "So you won't forget what I said and then get hurt. For love." But she seemed to enjoy doing it too, or anyway, she would get a look on her face that was almost a smile, a smirk, and then rap me one. Salome was six years older than Ben and seemed to be able to do anything she wanted. Mother let her have anything and do anything. As the last boy I got the least. But I got the inside of the house.

Ben hated spiders and Carl didn't like small spaces. Once Ben closed Carl up in a couch that turned into a bed, and I think that started it. Carl wanted to be outside as much as possible and hated closed-in spaces. I liked closets, and I would have climbed into the dumbwaiter chutes too if I could have. All I had to do to keep Ben out was say I saw a spider in there, in the closet or especially in the basement, and he'd stay away. When I figured out later that what they meant by me being slow had nothing to do with footraces, I realized that I needed to find what I could to make my own way. My two fast brothers maybe were faster than me, but each of them had something that made them slower than me sometimes. Spiders and claustrophobia, I learned, were not problems for me. I once let a spider bite me over and over to see what would happen. I got little red spots that itched for a while and then were gone. How could anyone think that a little spider or even a big one could eat you? Ben didn't want to discuss it. I showed him the spots where I let the spider bite. I said for a quarter, I'd find a big spider, or he could find the biggest spider he wanted, and I'd let it bite me. Ben shivered and said no. I said I would catch a jar of spiders — twenty spiders — and put them on my arm for one dollar. Ben walked away. Apparently he not only didn't want spiders on himself, but he didn't like the thought of them biting anyone in the family. I wanted to ask him if he would let a spider bite Salome, but he went away so fast I couldn't, and then I forgot later.

Ben and Salome had an uneasy peas. That's what he called it: uneasy peas, he said. He made a drawing of a big, unhappy pea-pod lecturing to some smaller pods that looked mighty unhappy, three of them. He said I was the wrinkly littlest pod. He and Carl were the other two. I asked him why I had the wrinkles, and he said I just did, that's all. And I always would.

Sometimes I wanted to be invisible and I thought that if I breathed in and out carefully I could find invisibility. I finally found out how to do it, but it wasn't with breathing, and then I took to disappearing from the family for hours. They thought I had run away at first. I would say I went with friends to the playground, went to the convenience store for cheap hotdogs, went by myself to play in the creek. And pretty soon I could drop from sight for hours without leaving the house.

The first time I went up from the basement, up the shaft of the dumbwaiter that went to the way-upstairs fireplace. I found there was a kind of ladder of slats nailed to the wall so someone could climb up there, so I just went slowly and picked my way up, testing each time to make sure the slat would hold. The lath was dark and seemed sooty and smelled like attic mixed with garage. I wouldn't give Salome the satisfaction of finding me on the basement floor in a pool of my own blood having been dead for three days and beginning to smell. Each time I went higher and higher until I had gone all the way up. Higher, it smelled smoky in there, like the inside of a chimney smells. I once climbed on top of our house and then up to the chimney to look in. I think it was when I believed in Santa Claus and Carl had been clear about the coming down the chimney business. I wanted to see for myself. Well, I looked down there and it smelled like cooked wood, I remember thinking. Old cooked wood. The shaft smelled something like that as I got up toward the top. One slat broke under my weight and splintered into knives of wood I could see looking back down with the flashlight. The splinters also looked like teeth.

After listening to conversations I would pull myself back up and try to remember what they said. It seemed "what to do" was not coming along very quickly, but I was patient. Salome was always telling someone else what they should or shouldn't be doing, always starting someone out in what she called the "right direction." "If you'll just do what I tell you, you'll be headed in the right direction. Believe me. Just do it and you'll see." Salome was very interesting as long as I was on the other side of the plaster from her. It was standing in that god-awful toe-on-toe, pinned like a beetle in front of the actual HER that I hated, the wagging finger, the hand on one hip, her skirt like a curtain waving in the breeze while she pronounced and pronounced word after word until I couldn't hear her, only see the shifting shape of her face waving in the air.

I began to write down the conversations as soon as I came out of the wall holes. I tried hard to remember what was important and write it as soon as I could, but always I forgot parts and added others I thought should make sense. I re-read these to try to find what it was my brothers and sister and mother knew that made me always feel left out and second rate—brown tasting. When I came up as a subject of their conversations, which was rare, I was always dismissed as some kind of stone-in-your-shoe they had to put up with. "Let's not tell Arvin and just go. He won't know, and we won't have to drag him along all day." "It's not going to be easy getting past Ma and going without him." "We'll ask her like it's going to be just this once. We take him along enough. 'Arvin's slow. Arvin's slow so we have to be considerate of him. Think what it must be like.' I get so tired of that."

I knew several things: I was "slow" was one thing; I could be invisible in the house almost anywhere I wanted was another thing; I could put things together if they gave me enough time; I could find ways to take enough time if people let me; there was nothing quite like the total effect of those meatball sandwiches they sold at D'Angelo's shack. There was more I knew, too.

The old house had become double. The rooms and rooms and rooms I grew up with, each child with his or her own bedroom or alcove, the backyard with its hedges and bushes that drooped into tunnels that ran everywhere. And you could hide inside or out. But mostly inside the skin of the house where no one else knew the passageways, no one else could go where I could go. I felt like a bug in an apple. I could tunnel anywhere and still get back out. Sometimes nails stuck through the plaster, but I learned to feel for them and bend them over. But mostly, the plaster was so thick pushed through the lath that nothing kept me from sliding down and climbing up the interior of the walls. The white powder left on me I learned to pat down until it disappeared. I listened to what the house said.

I found the box and what was in the box on one trip through the walls. I set out that one time with a sandwich, a cheese sandwich. I had learned not to put pickles on with the cheese or the whole thing turned to milky mush in about fifteen minutes.

I knew how to get to the *Moby-Dick* manuscript and had been to it many times before I decided to haul it out and see exactly what it was. It was in a wooden box that smelled like the forest when you scratched it. The top was crimped lead, and for a long time I just crimped and uncrimped the lead and thought of what must be in the box. Ben and Carl had been reading pirate stories a long time ago and sometimes would read the parts to me about treasure. My favorite treasure was rubies because I wasn't sure what a ruby was though gold coins were perfectly clear. Rubies and pearls. Salome had a pearl on a gold chain that she showed me once in order to tell me never, ever to take any of her things without asking. So I knew what pearls were. I didn't know anyone who had a ruby, but I found out rubies were red because of Dorothy's slippers in *The Wizard of Oz*. Once I could picture all the treasure that could be in the box, then I opened it.

I was disappointed, of course, that there were no rubies. No gold. I decided to close the box up again and leave it in the wall where I had found it and then pretend I hadn't found it yet and then come across it again so that I wouldn't be disappointed this time that there was no treasure. I pulled out some of the paper to see what it said. It said:

"And what do ye do when ye see a whale, men?"

"Sing out for him!" was the impulsive rejoinder from a score of clubbed voices.

[*I learned 'The Greenland Whale Fishery' in fourth grade so I sang it when I read this — "way, haul away, we'll haul away boys."*]

"Good!" cried Ahab, with a wild approval in his tones; observing the hearty animation into which his unexpected question had so magnetically thrown them.

"And what do ye next, men?"

"Lower away, and after him!"

"And what tune is it ye pull to, men?"

"A dead whale or a stove boat!"

[*I tried to picture the boat looking like a stove and couldn't without getting giggles. I looked up "stove" later and found out what it meant used with boat and said to myself, a-ha.*]

More and more strangely and fiercely glad and approving, grew the countenance of the old man at every shout; while the mariners began to gaze curiously at each other, as if marveling how it was that they themselves became so excited at such seemingly purposeless questions.

But, they were all eagerness again, as Ahab, now half-revolving in his pivot-hole, with one hand reaching high up a shroud, and tightly, almost convulsively grasping it, addressed them thus:

"All ye mast-headers have before now heard me give orders about a white whale. Look ye! D'ye see this Spanish ounce of gold?" —holding up a broad bright coin to the sun—"It is a sixteen dollar piece, men,—a doubloon. D'ye see it? Mr. Starbuck, hand me yon top-maul."

[*Oh, I knew all about doubloons. You bet. After rubies the doubloon was the best treasure there was. Doubloons were double something, twice as much, Carl explained and Carl also explained there were some doubloons in a museum in Boston and he'd seen them. Solid gold and you had to bite them to see if they were real, but I was never sure why the biting. Maybe they tasted a certain way and you knew then they were real ones.*]

While the mate was getting the hammer, Ahab, without speaking, was slowly rubbing the gold piece against the skirts of his jacket, as if to heighten its lustre, and without using any words was meanwhile lowly humming to himself producing a sound so strangely muffled and articulate that it seemed the mechanical humming of the wheels of his vitality in him.

[*But I used to do that humming when I was little then my whole family made me stop. Each one did it in a different way. Carl put his hand over my mouth and sometimes over my nose too and I couldn't breathe. Ben hit me on the arm. Hard. Salome tapped me with one finger right in the middle of my forehead. She said I had a third eye there and would learn faster. Mother sighed and hugged me.*]

Receiving the top-maul from Starbuck, he advanced towards the mainmast with the hammer uplifted in one hand, exhibiting the gold with the other, and with a high raised voice exclaiming: "Whosoever of ye raises me a white-headed whale with a wrinkled brow and a crooked jaw; whosoever of ye raises me that white-headed whale, with three holes punctured in his starboard fluke— look ye, whosoever of ye raises me that same white whale, he shall have this gold ounce, my boys!"

"Huzza! Huzza!" cried the seamen, as with swinging tarpaulins they hailed the act of nailing the gold to the mast.

[*Huzza, Huzza, I called too. I went saying huzza around the house like pizza, but Ben corrected me and asked me where I got such a stupid, old-fashioned word. I said I found it in a book about pirates, and he said, oh.*]

"It's a white whale, I say," resumed Ahab, as he threw down the top-maul; "a white whale. Skin your eyes for him, men; look sharp for white water; if ye see but a bubble, sing out."

[*A doubloon, I crooned to myself, white whale, huzza huzza. All ye mastheaders . . .*]

So in a way, I found gold—a doubloon—I realized later.

The paper was like dust packed back into paper form and the first sheet I tried to hold broke in half like a thin sheet of ice from a puddle.

I kept the papers completely to myself because I knew if Ben or Carl found out about it they'd have me get the rest for them or they'd go after it themselves, spiders and claustrophobia be damned. The reading I did about the white whale told me right away that the papers had to do with Salem, Massachusetts, where we had gone for a vacation, and I saw pictures of all kinds of whales but just one white whale. I knew the story about the guy who had his leg bit off and wanted to kill the whale. Who didn't in our part of the country?

I knew I had discovered the one secret thing that I could know and the rest of the family could not: not Ben with his tall certainty and long stride, neither Carl with his quick eyes and his tongue darting out when he listened, and especially not Salome with her... with her *handle* on everything—the way she handled everyone with words as if she were picking people up and moving them around with the noise coming out of her face. Especially not her. And not even mother who seemed more tired every day, always "just a minute" when I wanted to talk to her, always sighing and looking out the wavy window glass at something outside the house.

One piece of the paper—I was being careful after the one that broke in half—had a corner of a page just drop off by itself as if it couldn't resist gravity any longer. How like a feather the corner slid on the air back and forth to the ground. Then I began to think of the manuscript as a feathered thing talking from a long time ago. It took a long time too, but I read page after page of the handwriting with its open As I first mistook for Gs, the Hs and Ms almost alike so that Herman Melville looked like Merman Melville. I thought for a while that a merman had made up the words. I knew about mermaids and mermen and for as long as I could remember, living here by the ocean, and besides, Ben had been very interested in these at one time and told me all about them. I liked the sound of the pages easing into the lead box. I sat with the box in my lap and shut off the flashlight and felt the weight of it on my lap in the softness of the dark. A long time. Then I turned on the light again, uncrimped the lead skirt of the box and opened the top to read another page.

Once I decided to keep the manuscript to myself, I began to walk through the house among my family grinning with my secret. I couldn't help it. Once Carl stopped me in the hallway.

"Out with it, Arvin."

"What? Out with what?" I felt the secret rise up in my throat wanting to jump out my mouth. I clamped my teeth together and said, "With what?"

"Don't give me that. I know you. You have something you're not telling, and I'll get it out of you sooner or later. So spill it."

I tried to slide by him, but Carl stopped me with a knee and pinned me against the wall. "You're not going anywhere until you tell me. Just like the time you saw the cat that got in the basement, remember? You couldn't keep that from me either. So out with it."

I frantically searched my brain for something like the cat I could tell him. But the harder I looked, the less there seemed to be in my head. Carl held me pinned against the wall it seemed by magic. "The cat . . ." I tried, but I knew immediately by looking at Carl

that I wasn't going to get away with any cat story. "The dog . . ."
I tried then.

"Come on, Arvin. I don't have all day for this. Out with it. OUT
WITH IT." Carl tried what we both knew as Salome's "special
voice" that she used to freeze our blood and make us do things
immediately. It wasn't loud; it was just steel as if it could turn into
a knife and cut you if you didn't give in immediately. But Carl
couldn't pull it off. It was Carl doing Salome and the freeze wasn't
there. The knife was a rubber one.

My brain began chugging forward in the failure of the voice.
Carl tried it again, but there was only more time for me to get
ready for him. Finally I said, "Don't tell anyone. You have to
promise, Carl. Promise!" Carl let me go and we stood in the hall
and let Ben pass through.

"What are you two goofs up to?" But Ben was in a hurry to get
somewhere else and didn't wait for an answer.

"Okay, Arvin. What's up then?" said Carl.

"You know that place outside under the bush with the yellow
flowers? You know where you can go into a tunnel under the bush
and no one can see you? You know that place? Where the . . ."

"Yeah, yeah. Under the bushes. What about it? This better be
good, Arvin, or I've got such an Indian burn for you you'll never
forget."

"Well, if you go there . . . you can see everything. Everything!"

"What everything?"

"The Tillmans. You can look right into their windows and they
can't see you and you can watch them moving around in the house.
Mrs. Tillman sometimes cries, too."

"What about Jennifer? Can you see in her room? Did you see
her?"

I didn't know whether I should be able to see Jennifer or not. I
stalled and tried to guess whether I could avoid the Indian burn by
seeing Jennifer Tillman from the bushes. "I . . . uh. Saw her once." I
tried to read Carl's face to see if this was the right direction. Should

I keep going there?

"Yeah, you saw her. And what was she doing. Anything? Just reading a book? Dusting the furniture? Doing the dishes?"

I could tell that none of these would qualify for escaping from the Indian burn. I waited until Carl raised his eyebrows in another question. "I saw her . . . I saw her . . . peeing!" I finally said triumphantly.

Carl stood absolutely still for a moment. Then, "You did not. How could you? Can you see into their bathroom? No, you can't. They have that glass you can't see through on the bathroom window. I tried to see in from up in the tree . . ." Carl caught himself. "Never mind. You did not." He grabbed me by the shoulders and shook me, then thought better and grabbed my right wrist with both hands to deliver the Indian burn.

"Wait. I didn't see her *in* the house peeing." My brain raced to new speeds as the Indian burn began. "I saw her peeing in the backyard." The burn stopped.

"No. You didn't. Where was she? Why would she pee in the backyard? No, you didn't."

"Why do *you* pee in the backyard?" And I felt the Indian burn disappear as Carl appeared to be buying the whole thing. "Why do we all pee in the backyard? Except Mother and Salome. But the rest of us all do. Though Ben doesn't much anymore but . . ."

"Okay, okay. Big deal," Carl said, but clearly this information was worth a stakeout of his own. He'd try himself. "Don't tell anyone else about this. It'll be our secret, you understand?"

I understood and hurried off down the hall.

From in the wall I could also listen to the conversations in the house. Salome on the phone. Salome and mother. Salome with guests in the back room off her bedroom she had staked out as an office. And as time went by, I spent more and more time down inside the walls. My brothers kidded me that I had stopped growing until mother made them stop. I had learned to cram myself, knees to butt, in the wall openings and a number of times fell asleep in the dark waiting for the room to begin to speak. I woke up once to the whole family going from room to room calling my name, looking for me high and low. I hurried to the surface and waited until the boys were sent outside to look for me, and then I crept out upstairs and came downstairs pretending to rub sleep from my eyes.

"I was tired and fell asleep in the alcove. Where is everybody?"

Salome wagged a finger at me and made me sit at the dinner table.

I need a watch, I thought. One that glows in the dark or with a little light. One with an alarm I can set. Then I thought of the alarm going off while I was in the wall and Salome figuring out where I was. She'd spoil everything very quickly. I gave up the watch alarm idea but kept the lighted dial. I thought I'd look at the drugstore. But I had no money. Money had become the main topic of conversation in this house lately.

I never would have told anyone about the box and the papers if it hadn't been for one thing that happened.

I borrowed something of Salome's that I shouldn't have. She had a pen she got for graduation from somebody, I don't remember who, and she took very good care of that pen. She told all of us that we were never to use it under any circumstances. That's what she said—"under *any* circumstances"—and wagged her finger over our heads so we knew she meant business. Not just would we have to do the listen but something awful would happen to us if we borrowed her pen. It was the color of a ripe plum and the point was gold and there was ink inside that you could hear slosh around when you shook it. I think if she hadn't made such a big fuss I wouldn't have tried to write with it. Jeez, I thought it would make magic writing or something. I don't know. I don't know what I thought would happen, but I knew I had to try writing with it to see what the big deal was. I took it out of its box, like a little treasure box with purple velvet inside. I moved it on the paper and nothing happened! Nothing. No ink came out. It was like she had a remote control on it, and it would only work for her. It was heavy.

The tip was very shiny gold.

Then I tried to write with it again but pushed harder. Then harder. The tip of the pen broke apart. It just split like an apple does when you throw it against a wall. Then lots of ink came out. Oh boy, did lots of ink come out. All over the dining room tablecloth, and it seemed to keep coming and coming from some place where there was more ink than that little pen could possibly hold. I knew I was dead. Salome would kill me and put the pieces down the garbage disposer like she once said she would. She would chop me up in very small pieces . . . very, very small pieces. The ink ran out all over everything. There must have been five gallons because it seemed to fill the room after making the tablecloth black. The floor. The floor. Pretty soon it was like the ink was coming from inside my head where, when Carl made me feel stupid, there was a place that felt like it was full of ink.

Then I thought of the box I found. My secret. Maybe I could trade my secret box to Salome and everything would be okay. So that's what I did, only I didn't give her the box, just a few of the papers. She got mad about the pen, and I promised her the papers if she wouldn't hurt me. So she said what papers? Why shouldn't I chop your miserable self up and put the pieces down the disposer? I gave her some of the papers carefully, and she spent a long time alone with them. But finally she was very pleased and smiling, which for her was pretty rare, and she said she forgave me for what I did to her pen and the tablecloth and the floor.

Thorne

I'm telling the story like Ishmael, having survived it all and come back with the tale. I should have seen the whole thing coming. I didn't, of course. I didn't because we never do, do we?

I came to Newport, Oregon, a bunch of years ago, its university by the sea wanting a professor of American 19th and 20th century in general, and Melville in particular. I was a natural with my interests in *Moby-Dick* and all things Herman Melville. Newport had whales passing by twice a year, once in the spring to the north and then again in the fall to the south. When the fishing boats didn't go out after fish, they could take out whale watchers. Some had given up fishing permanently and now did whale watching all the time.

I brought my own Ishmael-like sigh, his November-in-the-soul business, when I came to Newport. Ishmael knew that it was time for him to go to sea when he wanted to knock people's hats off in the street. I know the feeling. But I thought I was doing it in a more professorial way. Maybe some emptiness like Camus' stranger, his outsider, Meursault, who can't grieve at his mother's funeral. My mother, on the other hand, was fine and living in Pennsylvania. My wife was gone though. I had put her through what I came to know as the isolation—a life on the outside of a scholar so buried in his work that he couldn't see anything else. I thought I *had* to bury myself in work; I thought that was what the life of a scholar was. I thought she knew that. I thought we had agreed . . . I thought, I thought, I thought. Shit. That's all I did, all I wanted to do.

There was a place in the act of scholarship, of study, that was furnished with particulars of retreat from the world. I think of that place now as a distant cave, not Plato's, with fuzzy lining. I could curl up in the lining and just empty myself out into whatever interested me. Selfish. Another way of looking at it. Me following my own nose. Self-indulgent—worse. And worse yet, self-righteous. Even more than a cave I retreated to, it was maybe a temple. And I was the high priest *and* the entire congregation of worshipers. I thought—and I use the word advisedly here— my wife should appreciate the cost of scholarship. When I was writing, I was hacking conversations and daily life into pieces that were useful for my writing. One of my colleagues called it "taking a broad-axe to your life."

I now appreciate the irony—Melville-style—that a guy showing up on my doorstep, my cave opening, my temple altar, with a few sheets of old paper in his hand, changed everything. Everything my long-suffering (and then gone) wife couldn't do. My students couldn't do it. But a few pieces of 19th century foolscap with scribbling on it began my return, my reluctant return, to the messiness of life.

Godalming showed up on my doorstep with his smirk. He asked if I was who he thought I should be—it was my university office, so I should be the guy whose name is on the door, but he wanted to make sure. Then he smirked and asked if I might be familiar with *this* handwriting.

He handed me one sheet of old paper with what I immediately recognized as Melville's handwriting, or a fine approximation, anyway. The part I had in my hand I could see was from the middle of *Moby-Dick,* part of the Town-Ho's story. Scholars, including me, have loved to speculate about how this fits in with Ishmael's telling. It was a "certain wondrous, inverted visitation [by Moby-Dick himself] of one of those so-called judgments of God which at times are said to overtake some men." The page had crossing outs, additions—all the business of Melville's creative process. I looked up from the page and the smirk was growing—almost a smile. He said he had more pages for me to look at if I was interested.

And here's why the actual manuscript for *Moby-Dick* would be so interesting to a lot of people.

First of all for scholars: we think there may have been some five thousand substantive errors in the first printings of the novel.

In 1851, copyright was a new invention—by the British—and authors writing in English could copyright their work in England (and prevent any old printer from making an edition of any work and selling it as in the previous practice). But the United States didn't have copyright and the old piracy continued. So Melville (and Harper Brothers Publishing) printed a one-volume version in the United States and a three-volume version in England. Sloppy typesetting on both sides of the Atlantic introduced errors. Broken type introduced others. English typesetters were notorious for drinking ale and porter at lunch and after lunch the typesetting became more freestyle: for example, if they didn't know a word or an Americanism, they substituted freely and called it good. The American edition was better, but not much better. And so scholars would like to see the manuscript with its notes and additions and subtractions to solve a number of textual problems, some say *meaning* problems. Scholars also like to see emendations to try to guess at the direction(s) that an author established through changes. Lots of good critical ink here.

Second: *Moby-Dick,* though the reading public essentially ignored it for the first seventy-five years of its existence, became thereafter the single literary center of American literature (okay, Mark Twain wrote that other center too in *Huckleberry Finn*). And after 1930 the book grew in reputation and stature until the great white whale sounded and leapt through school curriculums and the American imagination. Not until *Gone With the Wind* was there a challenger. In 1956 John Huston made the movie with Gregory Peck as Ahab. And so the work grew and the market for Melvilliana grew around it. Of many collectors, Maurice Sendak, who wrote *Where the Wild Things Are* among other books, was a fanatic collector of things Melville. The market boomed. What would the price of the original manuscript be? Anything. Start the bidding.

Third: the Newberry Library has the world's largest collection of Melvilliana. What would the tax deduction be if someone gave the manuscript to the library for free use of all scholars and other interested parties? Name a number.

And so I absorbed the smirk, agreed to meet Godalming the next day at his hotel to see what we could do about authenticating the manuscript. Oh, did I mention that, fourth, any commodity that valuable would draw out of the woodwork all kinds of unscrupulous parties? Diamond thieves, gold thieves, industrial secret thieves—they are the stuff of movies. Manuscript thieves? The right manuscript, yes.

But the second meeting never took place. Godalming was found dead in a portable toilet on the docks of the harbor. His body apparently had been in there all night and was being slowly embalmed by the pink stinky deodorant cakes placed in the urinal. The police called me about his death because my name was prominent in his daily planner. Only briefly did they treat me like a suspect, and then they asked for my help in contacting some of the other names in the planner.

I once tried to go out in the Pacific Ocean on a whale-watching boat in the company of other Melville scholars who had gathered at my university to chew over (yet again) Herman's prose and poetry. Eight of us set out and I alone—inverse Ishmael reference this time—wanted to die a swift death with my gastrointestinal system seeming to hang out of my body overboard with my breakfast and meals from several days earlier fluttering away on the breezes while seagulls snatched at the big chunks. That was the end of my career in boats.

I fished rivers and jetties; whales and seafaring I kept where they belonged for me: in books. At the closing ceremonies of the conference, my colleagues roasted my inept seafaring mercilessly. I didn't care. I was back on solid ground, and whales rolled and breached in the ineffable watery world that I would, given God's grace and luck, never visit again. Everything in its place.

In time, it occurred to me that my divorce too rolled away like one wave after another. I may have been losing what Melville's time called "the sympathies," or emotional connection, but the whole argument for domesticity had left me completely. I couldn't muster remorse or nostalgia. I still had the university library and all its machinery linking me to other libraries across the world, the Internet, professional journals, Melville listservs. I had connections I could control. And each day I felt more self-contained. The world with its wars and daily awfulness and injustice, its vicious layer after layer of fraud and con and deception I came to feel as some meta-text — not so much the main reality as a running commentary on reality.

And I did indeed recognize the homegrown irony that Melville wrote about just such layers, frauds and cons. But I found I could live with that irony comfortably. I think it was the distance, not having to negotiate the discomfort anymore, that drove me deeper into my scholarship.

Damn Godalming and his tasty little paper mystery. Here was something from my world of study — texts and textuality — that could drag me out into the glare of the world. I went reluctantly but left a trail of breadcrumbs in case I needed to get back to my desk quickly. Albert Jensen was another one of the layers it turned out.

Albert graduated from the university then began his career in local law enforcement. He had been through my 100 level American literature class distinguishing himself with main strength and brute force by which he subdued the materials, then bit them on the neck and consumed them. I remember thinking at the time that there was much in Albert I would keep and not trade even for a student of flighty genius. And so when he called me about Godalming's untidy death, I went along peacefully.

"Albert," I said. "Do with me what you will in the name of justice." He said he only really knew police procedure and not justice, but that justice, he hoped, was out the other end of procedure somewhere. I liked Albert, his sensibility, his proportion, maybe because I had so little. Nice kid, but I had no idea what he was getting me into—the biblical proportions of Salome and the Kraft clan, the many faceless manifestations of greed.

Albert laid out his plans for me to meet in a Seattle hotel with the people listed as appointments in Godalming's daily planner. The police suspected foul play in Godalming's case because of the unseemly juxtaposition of rich man and plastic outhouse. At least that's what I thought. So I was given a stock of non-committal things to say to get the conversations going, but I was never supposed to misrepresent myself as actually *being* Godalming. The police—Newport, Seattle's combined forces—would listen in and decide who were the sheep, who the goats. In fact, I had been feeling that way a lot lately and not having Ishmael's outlet of going to sea, I could only go fishing or try some heavy drinking with the locals. The Seattle skullduggery proposed by Albert seemed a plausible alternative. I would be in the world without my own identity. Maybe that would work out.

"Sit down," said Albert. "Be pleasant, mostly listen, then tell them who you really are only if they directly ask." Albert saw this ploy with convincing clarity, and I went along.

The two people who met me at the hotel proved to be of no value to the police regarding Godalming's suspicious death, though both proved very interesting layers to me. The third person I met in Seattle was not at the hotel, not in Godalming's planner, but was the pipeline to the manuscript everyone was looking for. And this third person I never told the police about. First two first.

I had the NBA finals on the TV when Gene Anczyski knocked then came into the room, and his shoulders grazed each edge of the door frame. I found myself staring at the second button down on an expensive shirt. He was about six foot eight with thick glasses that magnified his brown eyes, giving him the appearance of a near-sighted giant just wakened by the rattling of a beanstalk somewhere. His handshake swallowed my hand.

"Godalming. I'm Gene Anczyski. Let's talk about the manuscript." He shuffled into the room before I could confess my deception, and anyway he hadn't really asked if I was Godalming so much as stated it for himself. Per instructions I let him talk, and he rattled off a set of facts about the manuscript for *Moby-Dick* that seemed incongruous coming out of his big, square head. I guess he was establishing his credentials with me so he would be taken as a serious contender for the manuscript. Right in the middle of his exploration of the nuances of Melville's publishing history he glanced at the TV and said matter-of-factly, "Shit, that's no foul. What a bunch of crap. You can't use your hands on defense anymore but the offensive guy can slap you away and push off. The game ends up being a bunch of rich pussies walking around at the free throw line while the fans fall asleep."

I thought, Anczyski? Cleveland? No, Washington Bullets? Nicks? Ten years ago, maybe more.

Anczyski was a ray of light in his giant way, his square-shouldered, squared-headed Polish sort of way. Half of me went on alert—what Hemingway called the "shit detector"—while the other half of me was embracing this business, saying this is what I signed up for when Albert cajoled me into this deception in the first place.

I always took pride that in my business of teaching I didn't have to lie to anybody to get my job done. More self-righteousness, I know. I once met a guy in a bar, a software salesman, who said he lied to everybody he met all day—misrepresented his goods, fiddled and fudged and defrauded almost constantly. He said after a while it was second nature easy; he never gave it another thought until I asked. I gave thanks I didn't have to participate in that daily awfulness of getting and spending. I hate to talk on the phone. Even meeting with the book salesmen who came to my office made me go wash my hands. Avoiding the awfulness did indeed make up for the low pay in the professor business. God, that was a fine-fettled place to be coming from, it seems now. I remember it well but can't go there anymore.

I asked him, and Anczyski was who I suspected he was. He

threw elbows for a living for eleven years for four different NBA teams, then retired with some sacks of money that he put into a consortium with other players: modern art, apartment buildings in northern California, sports memorabilia and Melvilliana. All four turned out to be great investments with substantial resale value: the art speculation with sometimes fantastic returns for a good guess, the buildings low yield but steady growth, and the Melville stuff rock-solid no-lose resale but high initial buy-in cost. Talk about a bunch of words I couldn't string together before meeting Gene. Much of this came out later drinking in the hotel in Newport when he came to see how I was faring with the whole *Moby-Dick* intrigue. By that time I had begun to think he might be on my side and the reason he was in Godalming's day planner was Gene's reputation as a voracious collector of anything to do with Melville.

The whole collector world was pretty new to me though I had known the occasional passionate collector of Melville stuff when he showed up at literary meetings. In fact, Gene told me later a story about being a player between games and bored in Boston and reading in the paper about a Melville conference and going there to find interesting talk. I thought his boredom the perfect excuse for wandering into the meeting (and not incidentally having to pay the seventy-buck conference registration fee), and it was a kind of severe boredom that Ishmael claims sent him off to sea. So I started to think when I had been bored in my life and found myself parsing the word "bored," its reflexive nature in other languages (something you do to *yourself*—I bore myself with it). Then there was one time in seventh-grade math class when some combination of hormones and the real number system and the teacher's monotone actually created what I fondly remember as boredom-induced alpha-wave stupor. I later came to pride myself on always finding something interesting going on around me even if it is just the texture of the wallpaper.

After Gene Anczyski left, Jane Hunter came in looking for Godalming. She thought I was Godalming just like Anczyski had.

But she started differently. He had come in like a train pulling in to a station, like he belonged there and was on time. She simply appeared and fully occupied the room. I remember thinking she had her illusions completely under control and you could join her or leave. But there was something vulnerable too, some chink in the perfectly arrayed battlements. I tried reading her like a narrative, one in which she was a surface story going one direction while the subtext went the opposite way churning up flakes of irony along the way. Well, I thought that later. My first impression was more like witnessing myself as a walk-on in a Fellini movie in which no one had filled me in on what was going on in the scene, but it didn't matter if I hit my marks. I wasn't Godalming, of course. But the fact that I wasn't didn't seem to be material to her. My identity (I would get used to this ill use of who I thought I was) seemed to her irrelevant to the Melville manuscript, and I could be anyone I wanted if we could come to some accommodation about buying and selling. I didn't actually have the manuscript? Could I get it? Did I have a price in mind? Had I authenticated it myself? Well, if I didn't have it and couldn't get it, what the hell was I doing wasting both our time?

Actually she sat in a chair with her legs crossed with what I came to appreciate as her marvelous self-possession that seemed to flow from the way she held her hands up joined in front of her lips as if she were making a church and a steeple (see all the people?). I also found that move intriguing because it hid briefly her lips which she could then reveal and hide at intervals, having the effect on me of turning the lights off and on in the room. I played the part I had rehearsed with the police—no fraud but puffs of smoke and then mirrors.

She commanded the room: the birds, the waves of the ocean, tides—okay, a step down—the conversation, the direction to and from the Melville manuscript. She was the hunter, Jane Hunter. I was a gatherer.

In high school I had been in one play in which I learned that I wasn't very comfortable being or pretending to be other people; I wasn't good at it or even a little convincing. I always found myself, while delivering lines, seeming to look at myself from a little distance off and see myself being unconvincing. It wasn't so much failure that I felt but a sense of being thoroughly bogus in the whole enterprise. I admired those who pull that business off. I thought that first I'd have to convince myself before I could convince anyone else. But failing that . . . well, failing that, I found myself in the hotel room with Jane who seemed to not only know her lines, but needed to whisper mine to me, too. Jane was too potent a force for my pretending (don't lie, the police said, but you may misrepresent: I took this in a literary way to mean lie but don't say you're lying). Anyway, she was soon hearing my confession, asking me about my classes, my particular interests in Melville and whether I'd entertain her if she came to see me in Newport. I found out later that she was calculating that her client or clients, she didn't precisely know which, would probably support the drawn-out version of the pursuit of the manuscript rather than the slam-bang version that might produce nothing. She said later that she had to assume I was lying about what I knew because that was what anyone would do in my place, sort of a perversion of the "reasonable man" concept in law. Maybe a paraphrase: anybody would lie if large amounts of money were at stake, so it doesn't matter if you're a liar or not. Not much later Jane confessed to being puzzled by my inexpert handling of the hotel room situation and also intrigued by it. For my part, I had failed as a husband and become a scholar/monk out of inclination, and so failing at deceptions concocted by the police seemed in the scheme of things to be a negligible form of inadequacy. I suspect now that that inadequacy (and, of course, the very valuable manuscript) was what attracted Jane to me since I can locate no other charm or gesture I have that can account for it. Like an insect moving cautiously along a stick held by a small child, I had found the perfect venue from which to fascinate.

After Jane and Gene in the Mayflower Hotel, I thought my civic contribution to law and order (if not justice) was finished, and I could go back to Newport, and lose myself in my books. But just outside the hotel on my way to the airport transfer, I waited for the shuttle. A small woman with heavy auburn hair pulled back and tucked under a knitted hat motioned to me. I checked my watch.

She introduced herself as Mrs. Kraft and invited me to sit for a few minutes in a café across the street. She had a proposition for me. When I checked my watch again, she said that I would find the proposition extremely interesting if not fascinating; it had to do with the Melville manuscript.

"I have the whole manuscript," she announced as soon as we had settled into the booth. "Well, two caveats: not with me, and I alone am not the owner of the manuscript. But both of these in good time, Professor Thorne."

Mrs. Kraft appeared to be in her fifties or sixties without a gray hair and with skin that looked spotted from the sun but still possessing an inner butter-like plumpness. I asked about the manuscript first, whether it was kept in optimum conditions—it wasn't—whether it was available for inspection, whether she was certain it was the manuscript of *Moby-Dick*. And finally, why me? She held up her hand to the questions and said she would explain, and she did.

Her family, she said, had come across the manuscript in a lead-covered box tucked into the wall of the ancestral home. That's what she called it, ancestral home, without a touch of irony or condescension. They were willing to sell it but needed some way to keep from being taxed on the money they would receive. Again she reached rhetorically into the previous century to declare that the family had now come upon hard times, reduced circumstances, and the appearance of the manuscript seemed a fated solution to their problems. I thought how many times I had read the American 19th century for its worldview, its belief system contained in the euphemisms she was using to couch her family's plight. Fate, alas, the huge one. Mrs. Kraft said that she had given Godalming the single page to test the waters; he would have paid the price if I could authenticate it. She said there seemed to be a number of people willing to deal "under the table," in fact a line-up of potential buyers, and that's where Godalming had come in and now where I came in.

I suddenly felt that the Gene-Jane-Mrs. Kraft intersecting axis was offering an alternative to my life that I didn't really want, or at least hadn't signed up for. I had some experience with this kind of sudden accretion of the real world all in one place at one time.

My uncle committed suicide when I was fourteen, the day before my fourteenth birthday. He had been in a VA hospital for two years overcoming what was known at that time as a nervous condition, a nervous condition occasioned, it was further explained to me by my parents, by being in the army. There he had learned to gamble and to continue to gamble even though he regularly lost. I remember thinking how strange to keep doing something when you only lost at it. The whole business seemed surreal to me, though at the time, I had only a vague idea of the surreal. Now I contend that being fourteen was a thoroughly surreal experience start to finish, hormone to hormone sizzling through the blood.

But never mind the surreal, I received a gold watch for my birthday from my parents but it had no band on it. My father said it was a very good watch, expensive with a beveled crystal, a very famous brand. I wondered at the lack of a band but my mother suggested I could buy a nice band with my birthday money, maybe one of those flashy Speidel twist-o-flex bands they advertised on TV. I did that the next day and wore my man's watch proudly on my boy's wrist.

I went into my parents' bedroom for something in the afternoon, Saturday, looking for something that should have been somewhere else but wasn't. I don't remember what. On the bureau was a plastic bag twisted shut and then tied off. Inside was a leather watchband splattered with blood that had spread to the bag and made the plastic like a foggy lens smeared with red grease. I picked up the bag and turned it over knowing exactly what I was looking at—the band to my watch. The reason for the blood in the bag wasn't announced until the next day. My father's brother had shot himself in the head sitting on the toilet of the men's room of the Greyhound station. He had used a pearl-handled .45 colt pistol that he spent $175 for two days earlier.

The watch was a Gruen.

The business of the heart is confounded by the lack of currency. So we pay by barter. The trading is always just under the surface in this story since I had just lately rendered the cockles of my heart unto the gods of scholarship—what Hawthorne called the head-heart battle in everyone—and felt at peace with the bargain. But now Jane was stuck in my brain and even my knowing the great romantic literature of the world wasn't helping me any with her resonant, insistent presence—she turns this way, she smiles like that, she has one slightly crooked tooth, her legs cross by themselves with no noticeable effort from the rest of her body. In general I found the idea of her cumbersome at first because she was so obviously focused on the manuscript that any charm she radiated for me (and she did in yards and acres) she must have calculated to uncover the manuscript. I understood business. I still do. I just don't have much truck with it. And I can't seem to stay interested in it very long, even unto my own pension plan. I just lose interest. Jane was business wrapped in attraction, even seduction, then basted in elegance. I think it was the elegance that I found irresistible, so irresistible that I was willing to overlook the obvious roles we played as prey and predator. What about elegance . . . ? After a while I came to think of her elegance as the same as literary elegance—a collection of traits that went together so well as to produce a seamless effect. The best of Shakespeare, Milton, Dostoyevsky—Jane. I found myself taken in completely by my own musings. How thoroughly I fell for my own narration of what Jane was.

When she came to Newport for the promised chowder, I thought that since she didn't get what she wanted in Seattle, she had just moved the battlefield to my front yard. What the hell, it's just a bowl of chowder.

So the chowder went like this. We told stories about what we did when we were little kids. That whole era in our lives was pretty safe from revelation, from the hidden becoming the revealed. At least I thought it was when we started. I'm pretty sure, looking back, that she was way ahead of me at every turn. I babbled on about getting sick on a bottle of Mogen David wine that some idiot hid in the field behind my house, right in my secret fort. She gave me the missing piece of siding on her house in Indiana, then she gave me a V-8 engine block sitting next to her neighbor's house for so long that zinnias grew up through the cylinders. I told her how I used to lie face down in new grass until some bug crawled across my face. I was pretending I was dead and slowly sinking back into the earth, but the bugs always got me up and shaking. She said she used to love winter because she could pretend after a snowstorm that her house and grounds were beautiful and that the neighbors didn't have car ruins scattered across their yard. The snow would cover and disguise everything and make the world beautiful. I admitted shooting a sparrow with a BB gun, and my friend and I tried roasting it over a tiny fire we made with sticks. He ate some; I couldn't. She remembered being angry about having to wear a shirt when she got the first implications of breasts; she felt betrayed but didn't know by what. I told her my dog's flatulence was legendary not only in my family but along the entire block where I lived. "Oh yeah?" she said, hunkering into the one-downsmanship. "Well I had a cat for three weeks and two neighborhood dogs caught it outside and threw it back and forth between them until one of them killed it. I watched it from my streaked bedroom window through the distorting winter mud that sometimes rained down from the factory emissions and made the snow turn red. And there were wolves," she finished with a flurry and tornado hand gestures. We laughed and laughed and made up more things.

"Well, my father drove a cab and sometimes took me to school and all my friends at first thought I was wealthy to be able to come to school in a cab." Either one of us could have said this, but it was my fabrication, and I thought there were places I could go with it.

I couldn't remember laughing so much, maybe everyone in the whole chowder shop was laughing. We compared chunks of potato in our chowder in an instant contest to have the biggest piece. Then one shaped like a state. Then animals. This led to animal crackers, those to circus clowns, then dress-ups.

It was as if I had given up my insulation—no traded it off—in order to come out and play with Jane. We drank a beer with the chowder then went back to her hotel and drank in the bar. She had the steady drinker's sense to keep chasing with water. This led to peeing, to leaving me alone at the tiny table to think over what was going on.

The manuscript to *Moby-Dick* would have to be a frail thing, I was thinking, moving my drink around on the wet table. It would have to be either the American or the British version—the American probably. What had roped me into studying the great writers of the time was the damnedest high moral seriousness that ran through the whole enterprise of nation and literature building. If you didn't have a high horse to pontificate from then you by-god invented one quick.

I had a feeling that guys like Godalming still operated that way—the rules of the marketplace didn't apply unless convenient. I'm still not sure why my brief encounter with him left me a permanent distaste for the prick, way out of proportion to the amount of time he was in my life. Because he was a prick? Because he was rich and push come to shove really didn't need me at all. Maybe it was that self-contained smugness conferred by oodles of dough. I don't know. When I found out he was dead I thought, good, even before I had a chance to process anything more. It was like seeing a dead rat in a city street—the feeling that at least *that* one is out of the way. Later, I remember thinking that the reason I ended up dipped in the whole business of the *Moby-Dick* manuscript was Godalming, who was hell-bent on buying himself the best authority he could find to certify his purchase of the manuscript, to protect his investment. I was the guy who should change his oil, check the air in his tires, check the fan belt of his whole investment before he drove it off. More good reasons to find myself a good library and disappear.

And maybe my reaction to Jane was not far away from my reaction to Godalming but certainly inverted from "pissed off" to fascinated. They both roamed in a world I only knew by abstractions like greed, dishonesty, deception. My own world was characterized each day by me telling the truth or as close as I could get to the truth—wringing out the truth for its juices and pulp. But I proved a pretty quick study. Badly pretending to be someone else in the Mayflower Hotel was just the beginning of my re-education. Dissembling would eventually become easier for me so that if I wasn't in some fraudulent mode or another, I felt slightly uncomfortable. It was so easy, the transition, the slippery slope. I found myself misrepresenting myself to Jane almost immediately. I wanted her to like me. Oh no, I'm at it again. That is a gross understatement—"like me." I'd been a while without female company over the age of twenty-two, that patent sexlessness of female students in hooded sweatshirts. Jane was fresh air but air wafting all kinds of pheromones of the adult female. It took me a while, way longer than it should have, to realize she also presented whiffs of the world I had foresworn.

I kept thinking that—sitting in the bar while she went to pee—Jane seemed like a concoction in my life as had Godalming's death. She was one of the veils the world fluttered in front of my eyes so I couldn't see how everything really worked. And I was old enough so that I didn't want to see past all the veils—no Captain Ahab I. I had come to love the comfort of having hidden from me the gears meshing, the grease squishing out, the worn-out parts about to fail in the sore and shabby machinery of the world.

She came back and waved at me like a schoolgirl while making her way across the crowded bar. "And there's no sense in trying to do everything all at once," she said sitting down. "You have people to talk to. I have people to call. We need time to make sense of all this."

I thought, she must have rethought the direction of our conversation and now was coming back to do business. I nodded.

"And the time to put together a satisfactory deal," she announced. "My people want . . . well, frankly, they *want*. That's what they do. They want things and my job is to help them get what they want. But, Charlie, they WANT—out of scale with the way ordinary people want things. More even than long for, that kind of impotent lusting after what we can't really have. What most people do. Big-screen TVs. 'Oh Lord, wontcha buy me . . . a Mercedes-Benz.'" She laughed.

I was trying to catch up. Apparently while peeing she had retooled the entire conversation—cute though it was getting—in favor of focus and Janis Joplin quotes. I could at this point have walked away, I know now. Maybe I should have. I had my break in the logic, my confrontation with the bloody watchband, my way out. I didn't take it because I had the teacher's habit of siding with the question, waiting to find out what the inside of the proposition might be. I had not touched the sleek flank of Jane. I had not seen beneath the elegant draping on her body to the birthmark, the mole, the place in her brain she was afraid would open up and run all over my sympathies when she became afraid. Once she had begun to tell about the people who WANTED and wanted more, and sent her paychecks for her part in their pursuits, then I wouldn't be able to get out. I think it was that evening when I missed my last chance to skedaddle back to the library with a no thank you ma'am.

She laughed, and that's how the moment passed from one possibility to another. And, of course, I didn't hear the door close behind me or the other one open up.

Jane in my life was like renting space on a billboard; she was glaringly large and colorful and patently dishonest in her proclamations. And, of course, my shit-detector was wailing away that she wanted something and wanted it any way she could get it. My inner hermit said, fuck this. Then asked was I stupid enough to presume that she'd mix what she wanted with me and then I'd get a little of her, too? My inner hermit had long ago killed and eaten my inner coyote and was wearing its hide as a ruff on his parka.

But in the hotel bar, after the second drink, she floating back across the room, I found self-fraud attractive, even delicious. The light loved every side of her: when she bent over, laughed, slouched into her chair in mock dismay, tugged her ear, blotted the drops of condensation off the bottom of her drink so it didn't drip on her blouse. Pretty clever light. My hermit, crabby fuck that he is, bided his time. I could tell the hermit was temporarily *non compos mentis* running around his cave banging into the walls.

I remember thinking in the literary mode—that also came with a pair of drinks—words like hegemony and intertextuality and duplicitous text and self-referentiality applied loosely, loosely construed and constructed, loosey-goosey meta-application in fact, would, shit, I don't know what, explain her hegemonic intertextuality. That's why I usually stuck to beer. I could better gauge the speed of the spirituous vapors cutting the hamstrings of my reason.

And apparently reason, once its hamstrings were cut, went flopping off into the bushes that night. Jane and I (I can only attest to reason impairment on my own side, but I think the evidence is substantial that she gave in to suggestions whispered in her ear by gin-and-tonics) ended up in a heap of Melville scholar and mystery lady in her hotel room: arms, legs, tongues, hip bones, ear holes and the insistent lightness of being.

The consequences of the above business was that at breakfast we talked about dogs. She had not had a dog in many years and admitted to sometimes longing after the exquisite mess they made of your life. I kept thinking she was acting out the dog business to get at whatever it was she was getting at, in essence the manuscript although it seemed more complicated than that. But the dogs-business had its charm, too. I thought, fuck it, I'm only going on with this for a short time and then out. None of this drinking and naked and breakfast counts in my pile of things labeled "things that count." Anyway, how long could she want to do this with a guy like me without getting any closer to the manuscript, which she won't from me, until she pulls a gun, a poison ring, a knife, a syringe with truth serum in it, a laser saw cutout of James Bond?

"The dogs I remember the best were in the neighborhood when I was a kid," she said, holding up a forkful of scrambled eggs like a truck driver. "Free range dogs that belonged to someone but gathered into a pack in the morning and went looking for garbage cans to tip over like a bunch of juvenile delinquents. There was a little black and tan that seemed to be the leader, telling the bigger dogs what to tip and where. I wanted to be him when I was nine. Leader of the garbage can tippers. I have succeeded in my own modest way."

She waved the eggs a little and down the hatch. I was riveted, though I wanted to remind myself this had to be short term, maybe like a university quarter system, ten weeks and then on to something else. The waitress brought more coffee, the real stuff that, after three cups, usually made me finish sentences for people on the streets. Not an ingratiating characteristic, especially for a guy in a small town. I could feel the blither coming on even before the caffeine kicked in. Since this was short term, what the hell: blither, blather, blithering idiot, suave man of the world—all the same stakes. I creamed and sugared against the onslaught of my own frontal lobes.

She continued, "So these Indiana mutts were the princes of the street—"

"Princes of corruption and ill-use and scofflaws . . ." Shut up occurred to me but I was on my way.

"Streets that, by the way, ran to numbers and letters in that Midwest practicality of a grid," she soldiered on. "I always thought the dogs got organized each evening for the next day. 'Meet you on Second and B streets, and show up hungry.' Well, one day I saw them come down my street without the black and tan . . ."

The caffeine grabbed my tongue and yammered: "Who had taken over then? A big dog, I'm betting. That little guy pushed too hard on the big one and the big one ate him. Or in Indiana is it 'et'?" The waitress hovered between me and the Pacific Ocean with a full pot of coffee like a drawn gun. Jane studied my face. She shook her fork at me and laughed.

"I know what this is and how to use it, if it comes to that, Mr. Thorne."

Two "forked" jokes flickered behind my eyes and were gone into the neuron balls. My hand shook a little.

"So these dogs came toward me and my defense of our garbage can. I thought about climbing a tree and chunking rocks down at them. But they passed right on by me as if my garbage didn't qualify."

It was somewhere in here—the qualifying garbage, the leaderless pack of Indiana dogs, the sliver of a moon (no, I added that)—that Jane got the first hook into the cockles of my heart. Cockles that, by all standard measurements, had withered away to nearly unrecognizable little wrinkly things on the periphery of my superior vena cava. Lord, but she could play chug-a-lug with words.

She continued, "I stomped my foot, that's Indiana for 'stomped my foot,' and with my hands on my hips, I whistled after those flea hotels until I couldn't pucker. And still they went on, leaderless, the best I could tell. Headed for better garbage than mine. I was only nine. That's my story and I'm stickin' to it."

"But what about the leader? Did you ever see him again?"

Now she flapped bacon at me, no fork. Two fingers full of bacon.

"The leader? You want to know what happened to that little

black and tan? I never saw him again, and the dogs were never so organized again. But stories came to us from other parts of Indiana, especially from down state, where word had it that even the coyotes suddenly had new organizational skills. And a small dog was seen in and out of the maple woods at the edge of town." She leaned back and pointed the bacon away from me and took a bite.

I don't ever want to go there again, I thought. I should just tell her about Mrs. Kraft and get this over with. Jane was screwing up much of my newfound tidiness. I had come to want very few things, want everything from books and nothing from the store. And then Jane got silly with an elegant patina and waved her bacon at me. I think now that I could have gotten the hell out easily; I just said I wanted to but really I didn't.

We didn't have a band of roving dogs in my neighborhood; they all belonged to someone and everyone knew exactly who. Everyone cleaned up his own yard whether he had a dog or not. Dogs, like cats, went wherever they wanted. I thought I'd tell Jane that there was a collie on my paper route that had bitten me three times. He never barked, just trotted alongside me and then reached over with that elegantly bent snout of his and sunk his teeth in. I wanted to show her where on my left calf he had bitten me the first time and where on that knee I had collected the gravel, some of it still in there, when I crashed my bike out of surprise at being tasted. The second and third times I slid to a controlled stop. Mrs. Durban came out of the house the last time, and I informed her, while handing her the evening paper, that I would have to call the police and cancel her paper if she didn't tie up her dog. I wanted to tell Jane about the Irish neighborhood that started just after the Durban house and how no one in that neighborhood got the paper delivered. On some days some of them would buy a paper, I would have told her, from the small grocery on the corner where Mr. and Mrs. Fletcher lived upstairs and sometimes gave away candy if you bought bread and were especially polite. Jane would know that I was a polite kid and got candy almost every time. Mrs. Fletcher lasted longer than Mr. Fletcher. At the end, Mr. Fletcher came out from the back room in the store heavy footed and looking around as if he had just descended into that space from behind the moon. His nose was running and he made no attempt to catch the drip falling from the end of it onto the counter. He stood with his hands on the counter looking over my head out the front window. I held a loaf of white bread and put my money on the counter, but he stared out the window and said nothing.

I would have told her how I once tucked a peanut under my shoelace so the squirrel I'd been feeding would come closer and stay close while I looked him over with my eight-year-old curiosity. The lace kept the peanut tight, so he chewed through the lace and when I reached to stop him he bit my thumb—I would hold up my thumb here and display the V-shaped scar. Squirrels and I have had a special relationship since, I would claim. When one tasted my blood, all squirrels tasted me; all squirrels would know I had been initiated into their twitchy squirrel rage. But I didn't, couldn't, didn't get a chance to.

Instead, Mrs. Kraft introduced me to her family: her sons Ben, Carl, Arvin, and her daughter, Salome—the eldest—and their house, another character, and their slab of wood dining room table that had been in the family for two hundred years.

Arvin

Once Salome had the papers I knew I would never see them again. That was why I only gave her some of them. I carefully wrapped up the rest in a big plastic bag. I gave her the old box with the bendy lead foil they had been sealed in. I knew she'd like the box: almost black from being old, hard like the basement beams so I couldn't dent it with my fingernail, the lead part attached with tiny tacks in a tight row so they looked like sewing. And everything felt as dry as the air that comes from the bathroom heater, the one built into the wall with the big copper frame and the ceramic dial with only "off" written on it. The paper was like soda crackers. The top sheet cracked in half when I tried to pick it up, and lower in the stack they weren't so yellow but just as cracky, like thin ice or mummy wrappings. I went to the museum once with my class and saw the mummy wrappings. The pages were like that. Carl and Ben I didn't even tell about the whole deal—the pen, the box, the papers.

When I listened in the walls I learned what they really thought of me. I should have known from the meatball sandwiches.

D'Angelo's meatball sandwiches came from a dark green shack about a mile from our house, closer to downtown where the streets got dirty and the traffic started. Carl and Ben would come back from walking there and sit in the backyard and eat a whole meatball sandwich each and not give me a bite. They said you had to be older to eat these, like drinking alcohol or getting a driver's license, but you didn't have to be that old, but older just the same. Older than I was, anyway. Once when they had gone, I went into the garbage where they had thrown the paper wrappers. I uncrinkled one and licked the sauce off. Just like the pen when Salome told me not to touch it, never to touch it, I found it hard to stop licking the paper and then I ate some of the paper where the sauce had soaked in, and then I ate the rest of the paper and found the other one and ate that too.

Carl and Ben each had, they explained, rights to the furniture, rights that went back before I was born, and they got to look for money in the couches and chairs. I didn't. I was born too late. All the furniture was taken by the time I came along, explained Ben. Carl said that's just the way life is sometimes. Sometimes all the furniture is taken, and he'd look at Ben and I could tell they were trying not to laugh. So they got all the change that fell out of guest's pockets or wherever it came from. Quarters and half dollars even. Lots of pennies and some nickels and dimes. More dimes than nickels, they showed me, but Ben admitted he couldn't account for that fact except maybe the dimes were thinner and fell out of pockets easier. But all the hunting grounds were spoken for— that's how Carl put it. He talked that way all the time; he loved cowboys and Indians. We all three had been getting allowances but that had stopped and Salome said things were tight and we'd have to work to get money. Ben cut lawns for neighbors, Carl sometimes babysat and saved old newspapers until he had enough to sell. I wanted to walk people's dogs or help Ben and Carl but everyone said I wasn't old enough for any of that. So I had no money except what I could steal from Carl's hunting ground in the sofa in the upstairs hallway that almost never had anything in it because no guests ever went up there to sit. Money there would have to come from Ben or Carl themselves or Salome—fat chance. Mother never wore pants.

One day I found a dollar bill. I think the paperboy dropped it when he was collecting for the paper, and it fell out of his pocket or something and ended up in a wad caught in the bush next to the front steps. I found it—finders keepers, this was Ben and Carl's furniture motto—and I was half-way to a D'Angelo's meatball sandwich. Then some neighbors wanted me to feed their dog while they were gone, but Salome said I had to do it with Carl and split the money too because I might forget to do it. Carl took more than half because he said he had to do all the hard part—the remembering everyday and I only did the spooning the food part. After that I got some more money, and then I had enough.

I walked to D'Angelo's and got the meatball sandwich. It had six meatballs in a row on a bun that had been hollowed out to keep the tomato sauce in, and then they melted cheese on the top in a special hot place. As I walked away from the shack eating my first bite, Ben and Carl came down the street and though I tried to duck into the bushes, they saw me. They each insisted that they should get a bite and a good brother would give them a bite without complaining. I said I didn't remember getting a bite from them, just the story about not being old enough which didn't turn out to be true when I asked Mr. D'Angelo about it. He said my brothers were just having fun with me and not to believe everything they told me. Well, they each had a bite big enough so that when I got the meatball sandwich back there was just one more bite left. That's why I left Ben and Carl out of my discovery of the papers.

The next time I saved enough money to buy a meatball sandwich, I bought it when I was sure the bite-takers would be nowhere around. It takes me a while to figure some things out, but eventually I do and then I figure it out all the way. That's always been my way—not a fast thinker, but an all-the-way thinker.

Salome said I wasn't to talk about the papers to anyone, but she talked about the papers to mother. I went inside the walls one time to get away from Ben and Carl and I heard Salome talking to mother about how valuable the papers might be. She said there were lots of pages missing but what was there might be worth a lot of money and it could solve "our little problem." That's what she called it. I thought at first that she might mean me, "our little problem." But no, mother said probably they could send off part of the papers and see what they were worth and then borrow money against their value, or sell them or something else, I don't remember what, to make the construction business go again. Salome and mother ran a business my father must have started and Ben and Carl weren't old enough yet to take over. They made driveways and walls and sometimes swimming pools but not too many swimming pools because I heard Salome saying once that she wished we had lots more pools to build because there was good money in those.

Sidewalks too. They took me once to see the men digging up the old brick sidewalks that had been lifted by tree roots into little sidewalk mountains that were supposed to be dangerous or something. Personally I like to run up these and jump off, but our company replaced lots of these mountains with smooth brick again in the old Boston neighborhoods. And no matter how many sidewalks or retaining walls our company did, there was never enough money. Salome talked about borrowing all the money she could to make payroll and taxes. My papers could make a lot of problems go away, it seemed. I kept thinking, cramped there in the wall, that if I hadn't borrowed Salome's pen and tried to write with it and then broke it, I might have been able to keep the papers for myself and had meatball sandwiches for breakfast, lunch, and dinner. I could have had Mr. D'Angelo deliver the sandwiches right to our house like the pizza people do with the money I would get for the papers. I would have given Ben and Carl a free one each on their birthdays and free ones when I treated the family to dinner meatballs once in a while at home. I believe Mr. D'Angelo makes the finest meatball sandwiches on earth, though I haven't had any other ones except mother's, who when she made what she called Italian meatballs for spaghetti, came up with a pretty awful version of Mr. D'Angelo's. She said afterward that since we weren't Italian, the meatballs hadn't been as good as they could have been. She also mentioned Swedish meatballs, but I never had any of those, and at first I heard "sweetish" meatballs and didn't think those would be any good. Maybe they had candy inside.

From inside the wall I learned lots of things: that our family had money problems, which I understood completely, not having any rights to scrounge furniture and so money problems of my own. And then I learned that mother worried about what would become of me because she said to Salome that Ben and Carl and her could always go off and do something else but that poor Arvin, that's the first time I heard her say that, *poor Arvin*, would always be in a fight to make it on his own. I wanted to knock on the wall and yell, no, no I won't have any problems making it on my own. Just give me time and I'll be fine. You'll see. But of course I didn't. And I knew I still had more of the papers, much more, than I'd given Salome, so I hunkered down in the wall, and poor Arvin started thinking about how not to be poor Arvin ever again. I was fifteen years old; Ben was twenty-five, Carl twenty-three, Salome thirty-three and our family was in financial trouble that Salome thought might be solved by the papers—the part she had, anyway. I thought if that part solved our problems as a family, then the part I kept back would solve my meatball-sandwich problems for the rest of my life.

When I was young we had a little dog; I think maybe I was eight or nine. Carl and Ben wanted to teach it some tricks, and they made a list of tricks: sit up, speak, shake hands, stand on its back legs and walk, fetch anything they said. We had been to a circus and watched the small, white circus dog do all these and more including run up an elephant's leg and sit on its head while the elephant rushed around the ring. Ben and Carl whined to each other about the fact that we couldn't get an elephant, but set to work on the dog.

They had named him Ritz, like the cracker, and that's what they used to train him—crackers. I watched because they said I was too young to train a dog and besides I might make a mistake and confuse the dog and then they, Ben and Carl, would have to undo my mistake. The sun was out, it was summer, it was a Tuesday, and it was a week before my birthday when I realized that the dog and I had a lot in common.

I had been watching them repeat everything so the dog could get an idea of what they wanted. They'd lift his front paws and then let go and if he stayed up he'd get a part of a cracker. After enough times they just had to lift a hand in front of him and say "up" and he'd do it to get the cracker. I watched this business all afternoon. Sometimes they'd let the dog rest and run around and then make him do the whole bunch of tricks again, each with a word and a hand signal. They had a book they'd found in the public library about how to. While I watched I found myself wanting to do what they asked Ritz to do. I wanted to be Ritz or maybe Ritz the second and show them how fast I could do what they wanted: sit, walk on my hind legs, shake—everything. I would do it with or without crackers just to show Ritz and Ben and Carl how well I learned the tricks. I found myself thinking maybe a dog suit that could fool my brothers and I'd come up the street while they were training Ritz and then I'd wander into the yard and find them and then show them how fast I could do what they wanted. I knew there was no dog suit that could fool them, but I thought anyway that I could be a better Ritz than Ritz, and I watched that sunny Tuesday how the shadows got longer in the afternoon and the dog got better at his tricks and how relentless Ben and Carl were about training and how I was a dog in more and more ways the longer the afternoon went on. I sat under the tree in the shade, and when they finally said something to me, asked me how I liked what they got the dog to do, wanted me to clap or something so they could gloat about how well they'd done, I answered them by barking. I barked and barked and ran around the tree barking. I had been sitting so long it felt good to run and bark. I barked and instead of blowing out like they tried to teach me a long time ago, I sucked in and barked. Pretty soon, after Ben yelled at me to stop and I wouldn't, Carl had to tackle me and give me a Dutch rub and an Indian burn. Ritz ran in crazy circles with me as if he'd had it too, had it with Ben and Carl and their bites of my meatball sandwiches, their making me sit on the side of everything they did, their damn damn fastness and my slowness. I knew I was the dog right then and I wouldn't stop barking. Ritz and I were best friends as long as he lived, ten years, then he got hit by a car in front of the house. He took all his tricks with him when he died.

Thorne

When I got involved with the *Moby-Dick* manuscript, my job got involved, the university got involved. I was the grain of sand in the university around which it began making a pearl; maybe I was the pain the grain of sand caused out of which came the pearl. I'm not sure the scenario. But there will be a pearl for the university.

My solace came to be Jane—almost a love story. And I thought that could be enough: all the things I didn't get to tell her, the things I'd get to know from her. She talked about the people who *wanted* as if they were a cult of wanting located somewhere, some monolith of greed who wrote paychecks for her when she did their bidding. I was never sure whether she worked for them as an independent contractor or was actually part of some organization.

She spent a weekend with me looking over her shoulder all the time. Godalming's death was still under investigation because Albert said there were traces of chemicals they couldn't identify. The police thought it might be some very sophisticated poison that killed and then chemically ground itself up somehow and was nearly completely gone come time for testing. Godalming was also, apparently, taking some course of treatments in a European spa that included injections of high-potency vitamins and maybe some proprietary stem cells or placenta concoctions. Albert said it was hard to get anything out of the spa people because of trade secrets, but they were working with Interpol. Albert seemed pleased with himself. He said "Interpol" very slowly and seriously like conjuring up something holy.

Jane had come to call again saying she was no closer to finding the manuscript by herself, and if I could think of some clue to give her something to go on, that and more chowder and sea breeze, she'd consider the weekend a great success. But when she arrived in a rental car, she insisted that someone was following her, and could we go somewhere with our backs to a wall and watch to see who they were. She seemed anxious, and when I asked who she thought they might be, she waved in front of her face as if shooing invisible flies. "Nobody. Or nobodies. But they're starting to act like somebody."

I asked what all that meant. She said that a car had nearly sideswiped her on the hill—she called it a mountain—coming into Newport, the long downgrade with trees and nowhere to go but over some embankment—she called it a cliff. The car had passed too close and then cut her off suddenly.

"Jerk? Asshole? Cell phone user? CD player? iPod?" I gave her a menu of possible bad driving.

She shook her head. "There were other things before that. I mean even before . . ." A shower wafted in and rat-a-tat-tatted on the chowder house window. The place was warm and steamy, and the bowls of chowder came with great lumps of butter melting under a sprinkling of chopped parsley.

I was in my period of waiting out Mrs. Kraft and her cryptic, "I'll be in touch." She, her family, had the manuscript. Didn't have the manuscript. Even if I had been inclined to tell Jane everything, there was no everything. And I didn't think it was time, anyway. Now I think I was trying to keep her visiting me, soliciting me. I wanted her to want something from me since that was how the whole boy-girl thing started, and I was pretty sure if I didn't have some secret she wanted, she'd take off, and I'd never see her again. At least I was convinced the sex part was fragile. What would the fancy lady want with the monk-like recluse? Medieval. Or maybe 16th century anyway.

We ate chowder with our backs to the wall on the lookout for bad guys. I kept asking her questions to try to figure out what kind of bad guys. There are all kinds, I said. The hurt-you kind that want to do you harm for something you've done or to keep you from doing something; that seems to be this kind. So what are you not supposed to be doing or what have you done to them? Then there are the inadvertent bad guys who just happen to be stupid and in your way and run you over with their stupidity. These inadvertent bad guys are pretty literary and sometimes get called fate or bad luck. Then . . .

She was not taking my clumsy attempts at humor very well. She was worried and glancing at the door. She explained that there was lots of intrigue, backstabbing and lying in her business—scoundrel stuff, not murderer stuff. But sometimes the stakes got high enough and then money took over and washed away all ethical or moral conduct, and fair became whatever you could get away with. No one had tried to kill her before, since she worked in a world of relatively modest amounts of money, modest in the collectors' world, anyway.

I found myself time traveling while listening to her concerns, time-traveling in the sense of characters in a Vonnegut novel—everything was everywhere at once. She twisted her dark hair, and the light followed the twists. She scrubbed an eyebrow absently then smoothed it again. My mother's people were worriers.

They were farm people in the early generations and brought the habit with them into the towns and cities as teachers and store clerks. I watched Jane dig around in her anxiety looking for a comfortable spot to continue her vigilance. My mother's aunt ran the clan like a broody hen, clucking to this group, those outliers, that wayward one. She showed them where she thought the pecking might be fruitful, where the bugs and worms hid. Jane needed a clan, and I couldn't get out of her where her clan was now.

I tried getting more information from Indiana, researched the snowstorms that covered the neighbor's junk in the yard. She came easily up toward high school then skittered off toward vagaries of college, how many years, what happened to her people? I knew she wouldn't let me inside without giving away some of the outside. She glanced quickly out the window and down the street and held the gaze like a pointer dog. Two men were walking together without talking, slowly coming up the street toward where we sat in Alamo-defense position. Jane took her hands off the table and watched the men. About half a block away they stopped, one looked at his watch, said something and walked back where they had come from. The other one went into an art gallery full of tacky whales and whale references. Jane seemed to me so alert that she was unkillable, like a superhero.

We never saw the two men again all the time she was visiting and probably cultivating me to give her more information about the manuscript. The two men had business—one looking at his watch remembered something he had to do, the other out of boredom walked in to look at whale kitsch. Did they split up and wait for Jane to leave?

After the men had disappeared, Jane got a phone call and said she had to go. I was left pondering the clean simplicity of library shelves again. Things to know. Things that could be connected to other things. Jane was just the opposite. She appeared and there she was. Then she had to go and there she wasn't. I didn't see until later how fragile all that coming and going was. She lived by the phone and its inscrutable insistence. Power came out of the phone and directed her life.

The evening after she left I drove north out of town to go out on Cape Foulweather for the sundown where the lighthouse cast a long shadow back from the cliffs and into the parking lot of the state park. I was thinking severed heads on pikes all around my fortress heart. Knee-high salal bushes rose chest high wherever they could get shelter from the on-shore winds. And paths zig-zagged up to a second set of cliffs where rock and cliff and bush jostled together in the high spots. Right there is where I'd put the ring of severed heads, only yet to decide whose.

I was drawn here as a kind of default position when my marriage gave out, after burying my father, when I wanted to look off far distances to clear my vision. The heights looked down toward the lighthouse and the view flattened the rollers coming in to shore from the northwest so that the higher you got, the more pacific looked the Pacific. The flat perspective joined the horizon with the 180 degrees of the ocean and the beaches glowing light orange in both directions and soon, sitting near the top of the cliff on a rock, it seemed that all perspective collapsed and failed, so that big and small were the same; near and far touched.

I remembered one late afternoon years ago when the sea was the same leaden gray as the sky and a small container ship came from the south about two miles offshore and sailed what looked like directly off into the sky. It was as if my mind fell into the illusion as the sun touched the horizon and seemed to skid into the ocean until I could hear it hiss.

I sat and watched the light go. Down the paths, off the cliff tops, and finally where the water held the last streaks across the surface, the light failed. I rose and felt stiff. It must have been more than an hour sitting, and I felt no more certain about what I should do than I had before. But the sitting had opened a clearing place in my mind where what-to-do might form itself.

Cars dotted the parking lot below. A few tourists had come out to photograph the sun setting behind the lighthouse. The salal went black as the light went, but I could feel the path twisting down the cliff side. I put each foot down carefully to avoid wet rocks. On the first switchback, there was a rustling in the salal and then a rush and a shove in my back, and I found myself staggering toward the edge of the cliff propelled by my own attempts to get my feet under me. I caught a toe on a dark rock sticking up in the pathway and stumbled over the edge into the short bushes just at the edge of the cliff and sprawled facedown half onto the cliff rock, half tangled in the bushes. I remember thinking, "what the fuck, what the fuck," over and over. Then I was thinking how cliché takes over all rhetoric when someone has tried to kill you.

I heard footsteps coming and struggled to turn away from the hundred-foot drop. I scrambled around to face the attack direction, but the light had gone now and my glasses disappeared somewhere in the underbrush with the first push. When I turned to try to crawl away from the cliff, my feet felt empty space, then someone prying at one of my hands and then the other, not finding both at once while I dug into the bushes facedown and kicking air to find some purchase on the rock. My arms were spread so far apart that my attacker couldn't find them both at once. He pried me out of one handhold shredding the skin of my palm. Then he went for the other hand, and I instinctively shoved the bloody hand deeper into the salal branches where the roots insinuated themselves into rock; I was holding like the plant itself into the cliff face, breaking fingernails by jamming farther into the rock. Then I caught a knee on something solid and lunged back toward the trail and scrabbled wildly to catch a leg, anything, to get to the attacker. But I grabbed air again and again. Whoever it was had gone down the trail and was waiting between me and the parking lot.

Both my hands were wet with blood, and I pressed them together to stop the pain. They came away sticky. I caught my breath. One pant leg was ripped where I found the rock and had scrambled back from the cliff edge. I decided to climb back up the trail to avoid another ambush. If there had been two of them they could have heaved me over the cliffs onto the lava rocks below. I remembered another way down by going higher and climbing the second rock face to get over the top, then down the back side of the cliff through the salal that grew tall protected from the winds. I could hide there and wait to find my wits. The attacker seemed to be able to see in the dark, see what I couldn't see, but I could hide and work my way down toward the highway on the back side.

I felt for the path opening and climbed higher, stopped to listen for steps. Cormorants and common murres nested in the cliffs and tufted puffins spent the summer here. The murre noises rose, deep moans, as I worked my way up slowly and sorted through the night sounds and saw darting swallows feeding against the sky above. No one was following. Not close anyway. I started up and heard a rock crash down the trail below. He must be coming up after all.

I tried to work quickly toward the last of the light where the cliff topped out. Just above, I knew there would be a sloping rock and then more bushes I could use to pull myself over the ridge. Not much farther, but I couldn't risk falling again and lying exhausted in the trail. I kept going down on all fours to feel the trail, and small stones stuck to my bloodied hands. I brushed them off on my pants, then went down like a dog again. I repeated the cleaning, over and over as I worked the final fifty yards. Someone was close behind. Damn, this guy sees in the dark, and I can't see shit. The murres groaned and rumbled louder as if I had penetrated the sanctuary of small dragons.

The last stretch before the top was open ground, nearly vertical, but with good handholds in the pitted lava. The lava might just as well have been molten for the way the rough pits burned my hands. I must be leaving a trail of meat for the seagulls to feed on tomorrow. I stopped once again to listen but couldn't make out anything clearly over the disturbed groaning of the birds. One last scramble up the cliff face and then into the obscurity of the far side foliage. The last patch of sky was empty of swallows.

Head down for the scramble. No, look behind. See him coming. I'm more exposed here than I had been when I was first shoved in the back. There would be no problem throwing me off this patch if the attacker were stronger. I hesitated, turned and sat just where the bushes gave out completely and rock took over unforgivingly. I could wait and make a stand here, see what this asshole was like straight up on the last good foothold. Stand the fucker down. I found myself livid with anger sitting in the dark of the cliff face. How dare he kill me! How dare anybody kill all of us! And goddamn it, *me*, here. The lighthouse poked its light out to sea but did not waste light on the cliff behind. I sat in the dark hating that sonofabitch whoever he was. And it dawned on me how cosmic, how human, this particular activity was — sitting in the dark hating sonsabitches everywhere.

He came up the trail looming for a second against the ray from the lighthouse, supernatural, large, not stumbling but padding deliberately up the trail as if it had been lit for him. I saw him coming, not hurrying, but almost ambling. I turned and hand-and-foot fled up the remaining cliff face like a scampering animal, fled so fast I seemed to fly the last ten yards and then hurled myself over the top edge like escaping from a flood, a falling tree, an earthquake, emptied of thought, and I plunged into the tall bushes of the other side where hollow led to hollow. The path was overgrown and a labyrinth of turns. I always chose downhill but still found myself in the salal tunnel Groucho-walking wrong turns. I stopped to listen. Nothing but wind and murre groans. When I stopped scrambling I had come down the hillside and stood panting and ragged by the side of the road. I stuck out my thumb at the first car passing, but they sped up, and I realized I must look like a blood-streaked escapee from an asylum. Where I had wiped my hands were scarlet patches that flashed in the headlights. My pants and shirt were hanging in shreds.

The next headlights slowed to look me over then decided I must be some accident victim and pulled over keeping me in the lights and blinded. The driver turned out to be a dump truck driver I had met one night drinking. He wanted to take me to the hospital, but I convinced him I had become lost in the park and tried a shortcut to the road and ended up falling ass over teakettle down the road side of the bluff. He had been there once as a kid trying to sneak into the park when they started to charge fees. He nodded about the treachery of the paths even in the daylight and took me home.

I sat and looked at the back of the broken TV and wrapped my raw hands in gauze and sat holding the coldness of a new beer without drinking. Severed heads, I kept thinking. Am I one of the severed heads on the pikes? Godalming and me? The weary round world ashamed of itself again. How could two heads more or less make any difference to all the revolutions of the globe? Was the wanting that Jane talked about so potent that it required more and more heads to feed itself on? While I was receiving the stigmata, the shredded hands, Jane was making the full sacrifice.

Jane's car was white like a tomb in the sun along the coast road, in the green pasture mired about a city block from grazing Holsteins, who, the farmer said, never moved from their spot when her car came to rest. He saw other cars going by but nothing unusual; no one stopped. He called the police and they found her with her neck snapped and concluded it must have been an unfortunate accident, one of those moments that dumb metal and rubber and grass conspire to fracture probability. From the skid marks she wasn't going very fast, and she came to rest without any violence except leaving the road for the pasture, one realm for another. More *Moby-Dick* blues. I found myself stuck without purpose in the whale of a story.

Gene Anczyski could have been the next manifestation of the *Moby-Dick* blues if he hadn't been an elbow-throwing hatchet-man in the NBA and surprisingly quick for a man who made groaning noises getting out of a chair. I told him that Jane (though I didn't fill in many details at all) had been willing to buy the manuscript, and she had died in an accident that might not have been an accident. It all started to seem so existential, as if reason itself had leaked out of my life through a pinhole, so that I didn't see it was gone until it had disappeared. I had tried to shake Jane out of my life when her body had left Newport for the funeral trip to Indiana. I thought what good would it be to even give a belated damn and hang around in might-have-been mode? I had the library-inclination again, soft surcease of books right out of Poe. And then my new, large Polish friend shows up, and I think I have to be careful about sending him into the maw, making him somehow the next victim of the curse of Ahab.

And damn if "the curse of Ahab" wasn't just around the corner right on the tip of a reporter's tongue when the whole business came out about two suspicious deaths and rumored existence of the manuscript of *Moby-Dick*. I met with a reporter for a half hour, a guy named Porter who hung around my office at the university and seemed to have gotten wind of the manuscript from Albert or someone at the Newport Police station. I had thought that the whole suspicion of murder business was going to be kept under cover. It wasn't. Small town police seem to have very little resistance to reporter charm. Something like that.

Gene showed up as Jane had—a phone call, an invitation, a fortuitous passing through, and, I believed, a lustful interest in things pertaining to Herman Melville. On the subject of Jane I recognized in myself the biblical-lamentations stage of my own particular mourning. Fuck this. Fuck that.

I was looking for ritual and ceremony. The two losses—one good riddance and the other a longing after in full optative mode—actually sat pretty well with my otherwise conflicted condition. Maybe conditions. I think, like Ishmael, having been through it all, I see now what I couldn't see when it was happening. My job has changed, having left surviving behind on Cape Foulweather, and now needing to process the whole business, make it palatable by rendering it as ceremony, ritual and metaphor. I'm telling the story not the way it needs to be told, but the way I need to tell it.

So Gene shows up, and I don't trust him, though immediately we have the NBA in common to bitch about. I wonder how passionate he is about saving the manuscript or if he just wants it as an investment. I assume the worst and interrogate, all the time wondering if I can tell the difference between a competent fraud and the truth. With Jane there was always the added mojo of sex, its tensions and needs, how it just takes over in certain situations. With Gene, the NBA was no true compensation for the lack of sexiness. And as to the truth, I lived in university-world where everyone had declared themselves to be pursuing the truth in its myriad manifestations—scholarship, academic freedom to engage in the discourse of discovery. Ye shall know the truth and the truth shall make you free.

Gene didn't seem to be pretending anything, but what the hell would I know about real-life dissembling? My problem was that

I was a man of some subtlety in my world of scholarship but a blunt instrument as soon as I wandered outside my expertise. I paid retail in the real world.

Gene sat in the hotel bar where we'd agreed to meet and lurched habitually from position to position; he had an antagonistic relationship with all furniture. He draped and undraped as if he'd found himself in a kindergarten chair.

He had met the same reporter about an hour before in the hotel bar who had asked him if he knew anything about a lost manuscript for *Moby-Dick*. The reporter just mentioned a wire service, not a newspaper. He said he'd gotten an anonymous tip that the manuscript might be in Newport or a professor at the university knew something about it and someone had been killed or injured or something and there was talk of a curse on the manuscript.

I kept remembering Mrs. Kraft's face at the cafe. That nice old lady with rocks in her pocket. Her implication that she would not be denied the restitution of her family's fortune, the return of the family to quality folk. Quality people the Krafts had been, and quality they would be again. Would she be capable of paying people to fly across the country, pretend to be reporters, raise hell and shove people around, then disappear? Well, what about the next stage? People to buzz Jane off the road? To scare the shit out of me by chasing me all over the cliffs? Where did you hire such people? Summer stock? Are these actors or goons? Are they the same people Jane had been dealing with on the phone? What if Mrs. Kraft were the puppet master for the whole thing, and only poor Godalming and goofy professor Thorne were the vectors to spread the staged cursed-manuscript adventures? Could she *do* all that from Massachusetts?

I said, "I still don't see the point of hiring people to be obnoxious reporters."

"Chum," Gene observed. "Like chumming the waters for fishing."

"And they get what out of it?"

"PR. Reputation. Notoriety. Press." Gene said. "Fake reporters—the come-on—bring the real ones eventually. They can't help themselves. When somebody smells a story, they all claim to smell it too. If the somebody's a fraud, well, who's to know? The excitement is real once it gets the juices going. Ahab's curse. This might not sell if there was real news. But the NBA playoffs qualify for front page stuff now, so Melville has a shot too."

"And say this business makes the front page. Big-time newspapers. What's the advantage?" I catechized.

Gene shifted, "The notoriety jacks up the price of the manuscript maybe tenfold. The difference between any old kidnapping and the Lindberg kidnapping. There's almost not a story if it hadn't been Lucky Lindy's kid. Then there was the Hope diamond that no one would remember if it didn't have the curse. The King Tut stuff."

We sat for a while to see if the reporter would show up again in the bar. Finally, Gene couldn't sit any longer and wanted to walk off his plane trip.

Out in the air Gene limbered up slowly, I walked next to him. He said he always thought a good conspiracy theory had a longer life than a good conspiracy.

At home sitting in my chair and rubbing my red hands together like a miser contemplating his gold, and suddenly the Musketeer feeling was completely gone and the feeling that I am in this all alone became overwhelming. I could hear the clock in the bedroom ticking, slicing up the still air. The buzz of the beer seemed to almost supply words for the ticks, the words almost heard in river water running over stones. This babble seemed to supply a minor drama to the night—"this, that, this, that, this that, end, it end, it, hates you, hates, you hates, you, fuck, it, fuck it . . ." I waited through more combinations, waited for what I knew must eventually come. And it came. Tick, tock, tick, tock.

I woke in my clothes just before dawn in the big chair. One arm was asleep and my hands itched madly. Who would be the next to get it? The two of us from last night were candidates, of course. But what about Albert? Why not the waitress at the chowder house? How selective was the focus of a curse? Could there be collateral damage? Right there at the edge of all my worrying this stuff like a terrier was that everything might be an Abbott and Costello mummy routine—curses and laughing that turns to weeping. I found that massive doses of coffee made my hands stop itching. But I had the mind itch, the metaphysics itch, the creed itch, the belief itch, and the no-sparrow-falls-to-earth itch. There were suddenly sons-of-bitches and intrigues and intimations piling up like cordwood. And I found myself hungry even after I'd eaten breakfast, hungry without ceasing and not sure I knew hungry for what.

Arvin

Salome said we were going to have a visitor, and we'd all three boys have to behave as she said. It was very important that we did as she said. Important to the family business, to everything family. What was changed? I wanted to disappear into the walls and hear the whole thing from there but she said we all had to clean up and sit around the table with our guest and eat some snacks and then we could go. Don't say anything. Don't volunteer. Just sit around the table and be clean, I guess. Ritz was long gone by this time, but I thought of Ben making him stay and stay until he seemed to want to stay more than even staying because Ben said so. She said the man's name was Thorne and I thought of the thorns on mother's roses. Carl used to glue a big one to his nose and chase me around saying he was a rhinoceros. Once he got me and stabbed me with it and it came unglued and stayed in my arm and bled.

The bushes outside smelled like the warm dirt they lived in. In the winter they lost their smell. But when the weather slowly warmed up, then slowly the bushes began to smell. I never thought it was a good smell or a bad smell, just that the smell was there in the spring, and if I was blind or tied up and blindfolded or poked my eyes out, then I could still tell when it was outside by the smell. Inside the walls of the house the smell stayed the same; even the temperature was always the same. The box with the papers in it I'd had to talk about a bunch of times for Salome. I had to remember to keep my part of the papers secret when I told her about finding the box so she wouldn't take them all. I knew what treasure was.

Finally one day, Salome decided not to show me back the box anymore and I didn't have to tell how I found it and where. She said I shouldn't worry about it, that she had it in a safe place in a special kind of box in a bank where nothing could happen to it. She said it was too valuable to have at home anymore. I guess she knew what treasure was.

Sometimes now that Ben and Carl were working full-time at the business, they would let me ride along in the truck, and I'd hear them talking about the business as if I wasn't there. After enough times I got the idea that we didn't have enough money and had borrowed a bunch of money and pretty soon we'd need to get more money and do more jobs but there was a lot of other people doing the jobs we did and some of them did the jobs a lot cheaper than we could. The inside of the truck smelled like clothes that needed to be washed. Salome had taught me to smell my clothes before I put them in the clothes chute and never go down the clothes chute either. Ben once held me by the legs and put me in the chute when I was little. He said he had seen it in a movie and that he wouldn't let go and gave me a flashlight so I could see all the way down. He pulled me back out and made me swear on a very shiny stone he had that I wouldn't tell about what we'd done. I think it was some kind of test to see if I told Salome everything every time. When I didn't tell, he and Ben took me along more times doing things they weren't supposed to do like playing in the deep part of the creek, and I liked that.

I was remembering Carl's rhinoceros when Mr. Thorne came to the house. He looked like a schoolteacher with short brown hair and an old suit. He was older than Salome, and he smelled like someplace else. He put his hands together like he was going to make a church—see all the people?—but didn't. He just folded some of the fingers down and leaned the whole church against his mouth and listened. Ben and Carl and I were clean and silent and sat with Salome and mother around the dining room table. There were Triscuits with little pieces of sausage and cheese on them, but Salome told us boys not to eat them all, in fact, to wait until she nodded to us before we took any. Mr. Thorne took one, bit into it and then set the rest on the little plate in front of him. Salome had made him sit in the chair we all knew squeaked whenever you moved. All of us avoided that chair, so I don't know why Salome made him sit there. I always got the feeling it was going to give out any second and splat me on the floor, so that's why I never sat there. Carl made it squeak on purpose all the time, and that's why he wasn't allowed to sit there. Ben used to try to sit on it and not make it squeak as long as he could, but it always would after a while anyway. Mr. Thorne didn't seem to be able to stop it from making noise. All the furniture had been in our family a long time. There was a bowl of wax fruit in the center of the table. Carl dared me to eat one of the apples once, but I didn't.

Salome started off by telling Mr. Thorne that we had the papers, and we had called him because he was supposed to be an expert on those kinds of things. Ben kept sneaking looks at his watch. I think he had a date or something. Carl was sitting like a zombie. He used to pretend he was a zombie and chase me around the house moaning and shuffling until Salome caught him one time and made him sit on a chair facing the corner and not move all afternoon. She said if he wanted to be a zombie then she'd help him practice. After that one time, Carl decided it would be okay if we were both zombies, and he taught me to shuffle and moan and play like a dead person. So when Mr. Thorne came, Carl went to his zombie place.

Salome said the papers had to bring lots of money because the family needed it, and she pointed us all out to Mr. Thorne, as if he couldn't see for himself. The chair squeaked and squeaked, and Mr. Rhinoceros listened to Salome while she went into a talk. She talked and talked like she always did at the boys: "Boys," she always began. "I want you to listen to me and listen to me carefully because your very lives depend on it." After that she went off into whatever she was scolding us about, wagging her finger above our heads and saying, "Do you understand?" every once in a while. And about here is where Ben couldn't sit still and would start shuffling his feet, and then she'd put one of her feet on top of Ben's to make him stand still. Mr. Rhinoceros sat and listened just like he'd learned the way we three did that. The better we listened, the faster the talk got over with and we could go.

This time the talk was about the papers and then something about lots of money and then something else and something else. I kept looking at Carl because he was closer to me in age, and I knew I could take some clues from him about when this would be over, when we could eat the Triscuits, and when Salome would finish talking. Carl used to call me "clueless" so I looked up what clues were.

If I found myself alone, even just sitting at the dining room table, mother would walk past, stop and ask where Ben and Carl were, and weren't they doing anything interesting? Then, even if I wanted to be alone, I'd have to get up and go find them because mother felt better when I was with them. She'd say, "It's so nice to see you boys playing together." Even later when we were older and Ben and Carl would say we weren't playing, we were . . . something else, she'd say, "That's nice. When you're all together, that's so nice," and then wave at us and rustle off somewhere.

One time Ben and Carl were making what they called contraptions out of pulleys and motors they got from an old washing machine. There was no real reason to make these contraptions, nothing anybody needed to get something done. But Ben and Carl didn't care. They just wanted to do it, I guess. They let me watch.

That's what Salome was doing at the dining room table that day with mother and us and Mr. Rhinoceros. She wanted us all to watch while she talked about the papers for a while—made some contraption.

Ben and Carl and their washing machine parts made something like a go-cart but flatter and wider. It was very hot that afternoon, and they both sweated and swatted flies while they worked. I stayed in the shade thinking about what I could do to help. I went into the garage where I knew there was an old wicker basket hanging up near the rafters. It was blackened and full of spider webs, and I needed to stand on the lawnmower to reach it. Even then I had to poke it off the nail where it hung, poke a rake under it and let it fall. I took it around the front of the house and washed it with a hose. No spiders for Ben. Then I brought it to them, and they stopped working and looked at the basket and then looked at me. A drop of sweat hung from the end of Carl's nose. Ben blinked because his own sweat got in his eyes. Carl held the basket up, and they looked at each other.

Carl said, "What would we do with this, Arvin? What did you think we'd be able to do with this?" He looked at me and then back to Ben.

I said that I didn't know exactly but that maybe they could use it for something.

"It's an old fruit basket, Arvin," Ben said slowly, more slowly even than he usually talked to me. "It's just an old, dried-out fruit basket that's been hanging in the garage for as long as I can remember."

"I know," I said. And I did know that but I thought since they were putting together old parts of things that the basket might be something they could use.

Ben wiped at his eyes and handed the basket back to me with a sigh.

"Maybe it could be something like the glove compartment in the car," I said.

"How are we going to make a clutch?" Carl asked as if I wasn't there and wasn't holding that basket by the handle like it was an Easter basket or something and all my eggs were lost. All my eggs felt lost. I went and sat under the maple tree in the shade. I took the basket and looked for something to put in it. It looked so empty, like Carl could make me feel, that I put a small triangle-shaped piece of two-by-four in the basket and that was better. They banged on something over and over and then gave up. They were doing something with a rope.

I remember feeling so tired, so tired. I slid down the trunk of the tree and felt the cool dirt. I thought something had come and taken all my bones out and just my meat was left lying in the grass.

So tired I couldn't keep my eyes open anymore. I think I fell asleep because when I woke up they were gone and the contraption was up on blocks with the wheels gone. I stood up and took the basket over to it and put it where a glove compartment would be.

I got that same feeling the day around the table. Salome making that guy listen to her. Me not eating the Triscuits with cheese and sausage. Ben and Carl as useless as their contraption. Mother propped up in her chair. Salome biting the air over and over, chewing her way through the room coming closer and closer to biting the horn right off Mr. Rhinoceros.

Thorne

My apartment with the lame TV and the couch so ashamed of itself it had to hide in rags, with the stacks of books not really read but assembled into piles like hillsides full of sticky notes where I needed to mine and extract—this is my sanctuary as ragged as Raggedy Ann and Andy. The elegance in my life was in the libraries, in the architecture of the university, designed to resist the ocean storms and still recall the history of knowledge of the Western world from ancient Greece and Rome to the present. There was a little classical reference here, a touch of gothic there, keystones and Palladian windows, finials and egg-and-dart. I loved the handrails of the place, the students hand-over-handing up stairs to classes where they'd be the best humans they were capable of being. After class they might descend into various hells of pizza, beer and slovenliness, but in class (postulating that they were awake for the sake of their own glory) they were gods lusting after more fire, more lightning, more immortality. I found comfort in the idea that the university always was, though maybe not in this spot, and would after me proceed in some form to the edge of the apocalypse.

Gene Anczyski was like an over-sized mouse that had come out of his hole to study me while I ate lunch. He came and went on no particular schedule though it was clear what the attraction was here in Newport. I had the impression that money was not a problem for him, that investments in northern California real estate coupled with enough years in the NBA had sewn up his financial future and left him, like Godalming, with time to scour the world for Melville stuff for his collection. He also alluded to other collectors who could be cajoled into some kind of cooperative effort to preserve the *Moby-Dick* manuscript if it should manifest itself—pockets of some depth, he put it.

I was between classes, there were reporters or quasi-reporters hanging around the university sniffing out the story—whatever it was—and what I really wanted to do was go fishing and take stock.

Gene had come back unscheduled, and settled himself in a bar just sitting there watching the tourists. So instead of fishing, I went where Gene had installed himself. He had just re-beered when I blew in like a native owning the place. That was my plan, anyway. I was looking for my own authority. I joined the unsurprised Gene at his observation post. "Professor," he said and patted the table for me to sit.

"'It was absurd that he should be killed.'" Gene said out of the blue.

"What?" I said. I was not amazed that this statement should come out of this sprawled man one-handing his beer.

Gene laughed. "Oh, I'm sorry. That's a strange line I've always loved from my favorite mystery writer, Eric Ambler. English guy. Died not too long ago. They made movies out of a lot of his books. Anyway, that's a weird line from *Journey into Fear*. The hero is thinking about how complicated his life has become—you know, intrigue, people chasing him. And he thinks that line. I've always liked it. A statement so obvious you'd assume no writer would think to say it."

"It was absurd that he should be killed," I repeated, pondering the possibilities. "It was absurd that *anyone* should be killed? No, that doesn't work. I'm of the opinion that there's a decent logic to the killing of some people. I think the key to that business is the 'he,' a man pondering someone trying to kill him."

The tourist trade had picked up and the bar was in transition from quiet enough to hear the floorboards creak to the noisy laughs of afternoon drinkers. Two guys at a back table suddenly pondering existence—how Melvillian could you get? I wondered how much of my hand-shredding adventure Gene knew about.

Gene said, "The way Godalming died, how close it was to qualifying as an accident, what the fuck do you make of that?"

My turn. "I have a friend who works the fish docks. He claims to have the distinct advantage every day of pondering this very question as he guts the tuna. He says he guts the ones who were on the inside of the net when it got drawn up. One tuna over and the fish is still out there swimming around looking for the next meal, the next other-tuna to screw — the full tuna deal. I would never eat tuna. Bad luck as far as I can tell. Just bad luck, the ones in the cans are loaded with bad luck. Wrong side of the net bad luck. 'One Tuna Over' would make a great song."

I thought Gene's nodding wisely to my diatribe was a little studied. I still didn't know what to make of this guy whose NBA rebounding record I looked up easily. I also looked up the fact that he fouled out of almost every game he played. Seems he either just hammered on other players or the coaches put him in to do that. In either case, he earned his pay with his elbows and muscle, it seemed. He stayed in town for a while and then was gone again like the Parsee going below deck in *Moby-Dick*.

* * *

An affair of rooms I figured out early on. My life would be an affair of rooms — libraries, classrooms, conference rooms, meeting rooms, and eventually bars. In some ways it didn't matter that I had found a university on the West Coast with whales cruising just off shore twice each year. The other world came to me through all the electronics I could use, through interlibrary loan. One university was becoming so much like any other university that a key difference was how well ventilated they were, how the doorknobs worked, whether the lawns were kept up. The internal workings were being homogenized at an extraordinary rate. Zeroes and ones were kings.

Still I counted out my most pleasant hours in the library. The times when the library was almost empty. The streetlight outside throwing long shadows in the window and up the bookcases.

The sound of the ventilating fan is snooze inducing. I sigh. The business of being in two places at once I had become used to: the book, the room and back into the book. The toggling to and fro felt regular by now, even comforting. It always left me feeling vaguely worn out as I imagine actual time-traveling would. The smell of roses comes in at the window with the shadows mixing memory that remind me of Jane—her tallness, the way she moved in her tallness, always moving and then about to move again. Her faithless dance.

My sigh echoes off the floor shine. I gather up papers into a stack and paper clip them in sections. The roses are relentless at the window: Jane, her mystery, her death. The library work-study student yawns as I leave. I want to stop and tell her about Jane and her loveliness. That's what I'd say. She was a lovely person.

Outside along the trimmed walks, the copies of 18th century lights at calculated intervals, the Beaux Art building fronts, the world I found so soporific—it all said yes to me. The realms of Godalming, Anczyski, Jane Hunter—all that action and very little reflection—had seemed such a strain at first. Then slowly, like a full moon coming up through a leafed-out tree and then bursting over the top, slowly I found myself bathed in the seductive light of their world. For a while I felt as if they were looking over my shoulder at the scholar's security and certainty, my love affair of rooms, and seeing it recede into the background as I was pulled forward by the lure of the lost manuscript. Some nights I went to the library to see if I could get all the way back to the affair with rooms. The razzle-dazzle of the manuscript pulled me. Even the Kraft family was exciting in its bizarre manner and called me away from the books. Under the light past the administration building, I wondered what exactly it was that I found attractive. Maybe it was the entire untidiness—betrayal, the odd chemicals found in Godalming's blood, the accidental neck-breaking of Jane's terminal drive up the coast. At my back the library was solid like a mountain I could return to over and over. In the world were chimeras and *duendes* and trolls—all that stuff I suspected was real as a kid, then found out it wasn't and then found out the metaphors were intact and the whole enterprise real as a knife edge.

I had learned to think that art came out of inner conflict, that the conflicted state was the productive state; the soul in conflict with itself sweated the juices of great art. But for pondering great art, the scholarship of inventive recombination, I always needed a calm island, a refuge. I thought beautiful connections came to me when I was completely removed from the shambles of plotting and politics, of calculating advantage and previously mentioned severed heads on pikes. I expected to shortly be going there to the calm again and that this sojourn among the fire-eaters would end.

Then I met the rest of the Kraft family. Caroline Kraft called me as she said she would, and informed me that I must come to the Boston area and sit down with her family to discuss the manuscript. She would have more pages for me to look at. And that's why I went. Salome was my unexpected bonus.

Mrs. Kraft introduced me to her daughter, Salome, in the kitchen of their house. A taxi had deposited me unceremoniously at the Kraft residence—I don't know exactly which ceremony I expected, but I remember feeling vaguely disappointed that there was no hieratical gesture for meeting the Krafts, the keepers of the holy manuscript—and I clomped up the porch steps like mounting an Aztec ziggurat. Mrs. Kraft issued me quickly through the living areas and into the kitchen.

My first impression of Salome came as she stood defiantly among a gaggle of kitchen appliances, stood with her hands on her hips not so much defying me or her mother but the appliances gathered around her. The counter behind her was a nest of blenders and choppers and grinders of all sorts, each with a serpent cord running back to a single outlet that contained a number of devices to double then triple outlet capacity. The serpents gathered at the wall in unison. The dishwasher was slightly ajar showing off its stainless steel interior. The stove had two ovens side by side and an expanse of porcelain between its burners; Salome presided over the assembled devices. I remember thinking whether I would call them devices or apparatus. They seemed gathered together at that moment to intimidate me with Salome as their queen. She looked at me.

"Mr. Thorne, I resent these appliances."

There it was, the word I had been looking for. I owned a can opener, a microwave and a coffeemaker. I looked around to see why she would resent them.

"These things represent to me what has gone wrong in our world and what continues to go awry. This house is from the nineteenth century, my family from the seventeenth in this country. These appliances are my mother's weakness from the twentieth."

Mrs. Kraft walked slowly behind her daughter and began washing her hands at the sink as if she had thought to begin dinner. She washed slowly and left the water running while she examined them and then washed again.

Salome sat me at the dining room table and her mother and three brothers joined us in a silent parade. It was all very precise, practiced or choreographed anyway, but short of ceremony. I kept thinking of the appliances and Salome's resentment.

I had come to be here at the Kraft table by elaborate invitation. It began with a phone message from Salome who left a number that was not the family number it turned out. She left a concocted number that acted like a post office box that disguised the real whereabouts, not to mention the wherefores and howsoevers. I remember thinking, with some precision myself, "What a crock of shit this whole thing is." Hidden identities, a succession of chicanes and chicanery, fake left and go right—I had grown older without growing any wiser, apparently, and was running out of patience and good will very quickly. Two dead accidents, two very different etiologies. But I went to go find the manuscript trail and bring back news from the far side of the country—the Boston doppelganger to my Newport: whales, just in case the manuscript people were somehow implicated in the accidents.

Salome reminded me of all the reasons I had renounced the world, all the reasons on top of what turned out to be my natural inclination for the renouncing itself. She was pompous and a prig and clearly had cowed her family into this reception. I thought they might be armed—the boys anyway—until one of them seemed on the edge of nodding off and another one gave the impression of having been overinflated and on the point of bursting. The third was Arvin.

Arvin in time would be become the great puzzle and knight errant. But there at the table he seemed at first like the family dog dressed up for some incomprehensible occasion. He was staring at my cracker that held a small piece of cheese and a smaller morsel of summer sausage as if I might ask him to perform some kind of fetching and rolling over, and he would get the reward. Salome had thrust the cracker at me in a way that demonstrated her social grace. "Here," she said, as if that were everything that could be said. I took the cracker and sat down on a chair that immediately began to complain, announcing its fragility so that I had to sit very still and guide my cheese and sausage toward myself. The light through old windows with the many mullions cast plaid shadows across the tabletop. The air was dense with light that was East Coast light, the kind Emily Dickinson said in winter had the heft of cathedral tunes. Our Pacific light had some crispness in it that came of traveling over water after water rather than land in the East.

"We are straightforward people, Mr. Thorne. That is both our virtue, and for some, our shortcoming." Salome's voice was low and even. She had her mother's luxurious auburn hair, somebody else's nose—maybe her father's. I looked around for a painting or a photo, but the dining room was decorated in dark wood and a bowl of wax fruit. "And, we are simple people—simple in the sense of clear and focused, Mr. Thorne, not stupid." One brother, who had left off checking his watch, rolled his eyes and let out a breath through his nose as if his patience were at the edge of running completely out. Salome continued, "We have the Melville manuscript." She paused, looking at me, waiting for my chair to squeak. "And, we don't have it. These two statements depend on your definition of the word 'have'."

I looked at the bowl of wax fruit and caught Arvin looking at it, too. He had slumped until his chin was nearly resting on the table, and I wanted to slump down too—in a big chair with good back light and a new book of Melville criticism from a colleague I admired. I wanted the hell out of there. I had that same feeling I got at alumni events—meet the professor—as if I were standing in someone's drool and couldn't move. A combination bad dream in which I can't move very fast and some impending disaster hangs fire and the feeling I always get at seeing the woman sawed in half trick—it was all patently fake and searingly real at the same time. What was it about Salome that brought to me all the shabby rubbish heaps of the world that I wanted more and more to renounce? Back from traveling the wax fruit with Arvin, I returned to her voice that seemed to fill every crevice of the room, the interstices of the wicker panel on the sideboard.

I thought she must have seen lots of John Grisham movies, because she paused and dangled her paradox in the air for what seemed like two minutes. Maybe it was just the creaky chair that seemed to become looser and looser in the joints the longer I sat. I expected any minute to be sitting on the floor in a pile of splinters and burgundy brocade.

She continued in a voice I imagined was the voice-change Lincoln used for the part of the Gettysburg address that rhetorically altered direction: "Now we are engaged in a great civil war, testing whether that nation or any other nation can . . ." But she said, "We decided some time ago to make sure that none of us could even get to the manuscript easily without the others, that the manuscript was so crucial to the future of the family that no one member could come into conflict with the others. Not a sign of distrust,

Mr. Thorne, but of good sense in a family with varied points of view." I admired her word precision, clearly something she prided herself on—no hems or haws, no ums—as if she were reading off prepared paragraphs. Mrs. Kraft sat silently looking straight ahead, thoroughly in her daughter's hands. The boys fidgeted.

Salome, Salome, I thought. There are so many reasons why so few people name a child Salome. I pictured her from a Pierre Bonnaud painting with John the Baptist's head dripping gore on a plate, she naked and poking him in the forehead. The offering of her body revealed, and to her uncle at that, for John's head. Kinky shit, Salome.

She continued, again, as if reading a text projected on the far wall. "Professor Thorne, it was our family's tendency to hoard, to throw away nothing, for literally hundreds of years. Call it a genetic error if you like. But each of us is afflicted in one way or another." She glanced at her brothers, her mother, to make sure I understood who was afflicted. "That habit, shall we call it, kept what appeared to be a worthless pile of papers from the Melvilles and Gansevoorts in our family when any reasonable person, had there been one in all the intervening years, would have chucked out the whole marked up mess. Especially, as you know, before say 1928 when Melville was rediscovered—almost forty years after his death. But we are not reasonable people, by that standard, professor. We are hoarders and guarders of what we think might someday become useful. We pack away things, even trashy things. So imagine for a minute what our instincts are when we feel we have something valuable." She paused to twist a strand of hair, a scripted pause and twist. "We are a family who initially had luck when we came to this country in 1720, merchants of some considerable success. Then, to make a long story short, we ran out of luck and have been reduced for the past two generations to construction." She said "construction" as if it were sitting on the end of her tongue with fishhooks protruding from it. "This construction world has kept us alive—patios, driveways, pea pebbles around the foundation . . ."

She looked at her brothers as if they were responsible somehow for all these insults to the family. "Not even buildings or highway bridges. But curbs and fishponds and parking lots. The value of this manuscript to my family is nothing less than the return of luck to us. We *will* be lucky again. We only had to wait out the ill wind. And *I* at least among my family members" — she paused and took in her brothers and mother again with a gaze that seemed dripping in contempt — "know what forms that luck has taken. Mr. Godalming for instance. A tragic little man with more money than he knew what to do with. More money than taste. A twerp, Professor Thorne. The man was a wealthy twerp." Salome took a deep breath, seemingly relieved by getting out the word "twerp." "His money brought him to what acquisitive people everywhere must avoid, hoarding their very own waste products as an extension of their habit of getting and keeping things. Our family has many such lower-bowel complaints."

I didn't know whether to break out laughing because Mrs. Kraft, motionless up to this time, hung her head as if she had been scolded.

She continued, "And Godalming's death was part of our luck. Do you know how much the blood pressure rises while straining at stool, professor? The rise is so significant that Mr. Godalming's particular form of death is relatively common after fifty years of age."

I waited patiently, having promised to listen to Salome's full story before asking questions. But I also was beginning to get impatient for Salome to direct her explanation a little more, bring it in from history to the present, and so found myself balancing on the chair to see if I could sit perfectly poised between squeaks while I waited for the full disclosure. A blue jay sounded in the yard outside the window like a hacksaw. "But Godalming's death was our family's luck, too. The addition of his insignificant life to the intrinsic value of the Melville manuscript became his gift to us. You might say he died to give the manuscript a ghost it didn't have. And anyone in New England can tell you an old house is one thing, but an old house with a ghost is a remarkable thing. Even a valuable thing, professor. Value added. If one life added to the price of the manuscript, what would other lives add to it? What about close calls, near fatalities? So valuable, public opinion, don't you think, professor? But the thing itself remains unchanged. Only the story surrounding it has altered the value of the object. Melville's manuscript became imbued with the stories: Godalming only added to the value of the manuscript." I started to speak, but Salome raised her hand and pointed at me. I was thinking how to add Jane to the Kraft's family reversal in fortunes. "You promised to listen until I was done." She wagged a crooked finger at me. "I hold you to that, Professor Thorne. The agents, the bearers of all this story into the public's imagination, the press, is still hard at work discovering more connections between the manuscript and the fact that things go wrong in the world. So where does this leave us? The manuscript is growing in value and will continue to grow as long as the press stays interested. My family will only retrieve the manuscript when the value is as high as we think it can go. Then it will be available for sale, but not publicly. What my mother told you in Seattle still goes. We will not sell the manuscript publicly and be liable for the enormous tax burden. We will sell to someone who will bring cash in unmarked bills. Yes, just like a bank robbery. We have lights to check the bills. We have the technology to do this. We will accept the money when the public can no longer live without seeing the manuscript, and whoever buys it may display it like a two-headed calf and charge five dollars a peek, for all we care. Our interest in the manuscript ends with restoring the Kraft family fortunes. It is of the utmost importance, professor, that you understand this clearly. If you want to see the full manuscript eventually, then you will have to cooperate with us in our plan to make it public. You must give up all pretenses to greater good or the right thing and help us succeed in this. We include you in the transaction because you are part of the story; you have a reputation that adds to the public interest in the manuscript. If it comes out of hiding it will be under your auspices. You will be its host, so to speak."

The more she talked, her long finger pointing, her precision, even the sullen silence of the other family members, the more I found myself insinuating Jane into this barbarism. I wanted to throttle Salome and then go home, find a library somewhere, a monk's cell, renounce all this. I get a living whether or not the manuscript sees the light of day, whether or not I sit here at this table and disassemble and assemble my sausage, cheese and Triscuit—my wafer and unkosher conspiracy of meat and dairy.

I sucked in some air and began, "You will never be able to hide the windfall from the IRS. If the amount were as little as say, a hundred thousand dollars—and it will be larger than that by some factors of ten—you couldn't hide it from tax scrutiny . . ."

"Please professor. Your lack of worldliness is showing. I'd heard that you academics lived lives of theory and abstractions, but don't be ridiculous. We, professor, have a construction company. Ask the Mafia. Ask the Asian Tongs. Ask *any* small contractor. There are many pockets to a construction company, even a small one. Many ways that dollars come and go. You apparently can't imagine the bookkeeping slush involved in our enterprise. It might take two or three years to incorporate a million dollars into our business, but that's a conservative estimate. Anyway, call the IRS next year. Turn us in. The inspectors would find immaculate books. I keep them myself."

Salome finally leaned back in her chair as if to survey what she'd wrought. I felt not so much threatened as decimated. She was like a clean, sharp knife blade drawing through surrounding logic. She had this all figured out. That's what she was saying. She had thought this out and the loopholes were closed. The contract was done. She was offering me a part of the corrupt enterprise just like Godalming had. What would it take for me to be the pimp to Salome's fucking of the tax code? How many Salomes could dance on the principles of a man of principles?

Mrs. Kraft sat stiffly on her chair, looking away from her daughter, over the heads of her sons to an indeterminate spot on the wall. She seemed not to breathe. Her sons fidgeted. I kept expecting the boys to bolt for the door. I pictured rays from Salome's eyes dragging them back into the room, her power, like a comic book cosmic princess, mysterious and indomitable. I saw Salome and me as the two living things in the room, with the others as decoys planted there with strings running to anchors to keep them from drifting. My brain was getting away again, taking its own trip, and Salome now in turns grew to fill the room, then shrank to a pinpoint of power circling above the decoys' heads.

"I tell you what," I said. "As a Melville scholar, what I'd like to see is the manuscript . . ."

"That won't be possible, Professor Thorne. You've seen enough to verify it," Salome shot out.

"No, wait. I'd like to see the manuscript made public in some way or another. I don't care how. And, worldly or not, I don't consider the 'deal' any of my business. I just want to look at the manuscript, solve a scholar's problems in a scholar's way. Whether your family becomes rich is not my affair. What can I do to help you make the manuscript part of the public domain?"

Salome sighed. "If you had been listening carefully, you might have detected your part in this, Professor. You are the person the newspapers will come to, *have already* come to for corroboration about stories. And the stories, curses, innuendo, ghosts, whatever will build the value of the manuscript, are all coming through you."

"You don't expect me to . . ."

"I don't expect you to do anything but think, Professor. If that's not too much to ask, is it? Take your time and think through each interview. Act as our agent, if you will, and promulgate the enabling narrative. Fill our piggy bank. Think of it that way. When we start to get offers we can't refuse, offers that put our family back to where father's people. . . . Well, just be sure that we will tell you when the newsworthiness of the manuscript and our, what shall we call it, our sufficiency? Our greed? When these come together, we'll make a deal for the manuscript with any petitioner who will abide by our guidelines. Cash, anonymity, etceteras. You will be our certifying agent. And you will document authenticity for the buyer. The buyer should find this worthwhile and remunerate you. You work that out with the buyer."

"I'm not sure what a monk like me could possibly do to make you more money," I said. Salome screwed up her face in disgust as if she had had to explain something too many times to a slow child. "I know," I continued, "what the manuscript should look like. But how could I succeed in getting the most money for you? I can't guarantee anything. I am not a person who has great use for guile in his work. I pretty much say it as I find it, say true things, or what I think is true, all day long. You need a salesman, a dissembler, maybe even a con man. I don't see why you don't get yourself a good, slick used-car salesman."

Salome flicked the back of her hand at me as if telling me to leave. It was certainly some kind of dismissal. "Just go and give it a try, Professor. Let me decide who I need and don't need. You just give this a try and see how it comes out. If you can't think this through . . . well, we'll just have to fire you, I guess, and get someone who can do it. But in the meantime, we'll give you a shot at making a little money, maybe even your reputation. We'll be in touch with you."

Salome stood and indicated the door, and the zombies awoke and milled. This family was what I got after Jane had come and gone, all in exchange for descending from the tower.

With Jane my reluctance to buy back in to the world had been overcome so quickly—her shoes? the drinking and laughing? the grand illusion that it was me and not the manuscript that called to her (oh, the power of that particular fraud)?—that now the Kraft family made me want to flee on the one hand, but Salome's

Faustian, and fustian, rhetoric drew me in on the other. Salome's dance.

I thought that, on the one hand, Salome was performing an organizational tidying ritual worthy of the manuscript, of the whole business. Someone had to do it with all the messiness inherent in this. On the other hand, I had the distinct feeling that I would kill Salome if I were someone who killed people. I mean, the metaphor of killing occurred to me with some vigor as she sat there and laid out the Kraft affairs and my role in them, waved her finger in the air over us all like some pontificating priestess. Her mother and brothers seemed to shrink beneath her magician's gestures. I found myself somewhat miniaturized, too.

I had wrestled with my faith, my lack of faith, long ago. I made a temporary—and that was good enough—accommodation to being part of the long cosmic view as strings of molecules on their way back to simpler states—the getting-on-with-it view I called it. I had no real reason to hurry the process along either, no itching to get done with the waiting that I imagine suicides experience. Now or later—what's the difference? Well, to me the difference was waiting for the next Salome to happen into my life. And, damn, if every time the new Salome came along I was at first fascinated and then found myself on the run. After the dinner table with this particular Salome, I was on the run.

Arvin

My mother always called it "wool gathering," this being there without actually being there. For me, a chance to gather wool was a chance to think about D'Angelo's meatball submarine sandwiches.

The few I'd eaten had never been enough to stop my wanting. Even while I ate one, I found myself plotting how I could get the next one. The meatballs were lined up in the hollowed-out bun, assembled by Mr. D'Angelo himself who moved like a cat, then he covered them in red sauce with its tiny pieces of green pepper and onion, then Parmesan cheese and then passed under the broiler for a quick melt. Even if I was sitting at the table at home, I really was gone down the street to D'Angelo's and was waiting for my meatball sandwich. The meatballs were small and round. Mr. D made them in a press eight at a time in the back, each one the same size as the others, each one to be fried and then ready for the sandwich.

My problem was that I couldn't afford these round beauties. Carl used to call everything "my beauty" at one time. He got that from one of the books about pirates. These beauties cost me my entire savings every time I could manage to buy them. Ben and Carl seemed to always have money from mowing lawns and doing odd jobs after school. I had to find the price penny by penny, enough money to visit D'Angelo's.

Once Ben had walked up to me as I was eating a meatball sandwich on the way home, and he demanded a bite. The bite turned out to be several monstrous chomps like a dog does, and that left me holding the rest in a napkin like a bloodied corpse. I wanted to cry, and Ben skipped off immediately to someplace else. He ate most of the beauties. If all meatball sandwiches were shared, it wouldn't have been so bad. But Ben and Carl went off to D'Angelo's together and didn't tell me. I could smell it on them as clearly as if they waved the greasy paper in my face. I knew they had as many sandwiches as they could eat. And then I pictured them, stuffed with beauties, fallen asleep under a tree somewhere. Salome and mother never could hear the call of the meatball. How could they? Salome seemed to live without eating anything. She'd push her dinner around on her plate making a mess of it so we wouldn't touch the disaster that looked as if she'd chewed it up and spit it on her plate. If we had pudding, butterscotch or chocolate, it didn't matter, she'd dump milk on it, stir it into glop and then leave it after the meal. She didn't seem to want to eat it herself. She made sure that none of us would even consider eating the remains. And her pockets were always full of money somehow, but I never saw her eat a meatball sandwich or even smell it on her.

Once, only once, I considered stealing money from Salome. Ben and Carl hid and guarded their money like dragons. But Salome's purse was always lying around full of my way too beautiful meatball sandwiches.

I could see the green poking out of her wallet inside the purse. Dollars and dollars seemed stacked together. Maybe fives, maybe tens. I caught myself drooling about what I could get. But I knew the price of getting caught. The garbage disposer. What could she do more than chop me up and put me down the garbage disposer? I knew that Salome *would* know exactly what to do to me. She always knew exactly.

And so I left Salome's purse alone and thought and thought about meatball sandwiches.

It was windy and the trees clicked against each other. It wasn't Halloween yet but it was coming, and I would have to put up with all of Ben's and Carl's, especially Carl's, tricks. Carl seemed to become crazier the closer to Halloween we got. He collected black string to make his spider webs that were really more like fishnets to catch little kids coming to the door for treats. And he had some air horns that he hid the rest of the year, except New Year's, so I couldn't find them. I played one, once, and it got stuck on and I couldn't find out how to make it stop. Then I put it in the garbage can while it was still going and going and put garbage on top of it until it stopped. I don't know how Carl found it there, but he did. Ben must have heard it and told him. I never thought I was included with Ben and Carl in anything they did even when mother made them take me. They had a way of talking across the top of my head to each other. One whole summer they talked ob-talk and put ob into words everywhere, and I couldn't figure out fast enough how to take the ob out and understand the talk they did. They took me along all right. They just never let me be with them.

Carl was crazy with Halloween but Ben was crazy with Christmas in a different way. He used to sit Carl and me down in front of him and tell long stories about how many presents we used to get when the family had more money and father was alive. I didn't remember, but Ben made it seem like we were rich or something and then something happened, and we weren't rich anymore. Ben almost whispered when he talked about the toy garage and filling station he got one year. It had lots of plastic cars that could gas up and go up on the hoist and men in uniforms who you could move around, and it said Texaco. Then there were the sleds with springs like cars have—coil springs and leaf springs because Ben liked to say the right names of things. That sled was gone by the time I was old enough or we had to sell it to buy food maybe. I don't know. I never even saw it. After Ben stopped we'd wander off, Carl and I, but maybe that afternoon Ben would call us together again, make us sit down and say he remembered more things from Christmas a long time ago, and we should hear them. Then he'd start again on presents like a miniature train set made in Germany that was way better than any train sets Carl and I had ever seen. Pencils that changed color in your hand, a gold-colored slinky once, but it wasn't real gold Ben said, and the Christmas lights had little candles with colored water that bubbled up, and they got hot and could burn your finger or the tree, and one neighbor left theirs on when they went away, and there was a big fire. Ben liked telling about what kind of decorations we had then and don't have now. Salome stopped and listened once for a while and then said, "Stop it Ben. They don't know what's true or not true when you say those things. So just stop it." And then she walked away and took all the air out of the room, too.

So Carl had Halloween and Ben had Christmas. I thought I should have a holiday too, but I couldn't decide because I really liked the same ones they did, but I knew I couldn't say that or they'd both roll their eyes not saying what I knew they were thinking, that I was a fool. I thought for a while that I'd take the 4th of July but the more I thought about it the more I didn't really like the 4th because my brothers always got firecrackers somewhere and spent a lot of time trying to make me jump. They also taped fireworks together and tried to make bigger deals out of the ones we could buy, which were *not* illegal, but by taping some together they could make something that might be illegal if anybody thought about it. I usually tried to go somewhere by myself when they got to taping because of the one time when part of the thing they made flew off and almost hit me and started the garage shingles on fire, and they had to use the hose to stop the fire.

So finally I decided to start my own holiday and not tell anyone about it and celebrate it myself. It had to be in the summer. I called it Brown Dog Day because it sounded a little like Ground Hog Day, and I never really got what was interesting at all about that holiday.

Brown Dog Day was two weeks after the 4th of July, exactly two weeks. It was about brown dogs, and that was as far as I thought it out at first. I liked to say Brown Dog Day, Brown Dog Day while walking along and say it in rhythm with my walking. And part of the fun was not telling Ben and Carl a single thing about it. After a while I added the decoration part. I would find brown dogs and decorate them if I could get them to come to me. Most would come unless they were tied in someone's backyard and just barked and barked. I got red and white crepe paper and tied on little pieces wrapped together and let the dogs go on their way. I also decided that dogs with a little brown on them counted and deserved decoration, too. But not all-black dogs or all-white dogs, but those butterscotch-pudding colored ones, those cocker spaniels from down the street, were okay to decorate. I could be very pleased to see most of the dogs in the neighborhood with a little decoration on them on Brown Dog Day. They looked good.

So when I found those papers inside the house, it was the same time people started wearing camo. At first I didn't understand camo. And I wasn't feeling like being a fool for Ben and Carl, so I just watched and waited for the camo business to make sense. I did the same thing with the papers—waited until I could make sense out of them, but then the thing happened with Salome's pen, and I had to give her some of them. But between camo and the papers I learned about how long it took for me to figure things out, and I knew that I'd always have to wait about that long when the stuff of the world puzzled me.

Camo first. I saw camo, the regular green and brown and black version, before the mossy oak breakup and the other fancy ones, the black and white, the orange and black. I don't know. I thought, why would someone want clothes like that? I asked Ben first thinking I might get a short answer that would make sense. Carl usually answered anything he thought I was clueless about by starting near the beginning of the world and then including pirates and some war scenes and what-all. So, I asked Ben, and like I thought he gave a quick answer. And useless. People wear camo to hide. He said it was camouflage really and that meant to hide something. Then he walked off.

Next time I saw camo was on a neighbor, a T-shirt. I didn't get the hiding part. Where would he be that would look like the colors he was wearing? Someplace green and brown and black. I didn't know any place like that. I was thinking I might have to go to Carl for the long version of camo when a catalog came to our house in the fall. I looked through it at the pictures, and then I saw a whole bedroom decorated in camo with a quilt, and chair coverings and a rug. A whole camo room. Now the mystery became deeper. I thought I was getting the idea maybe about hiding out in some green-brown-black place and then I found the place. It was a room. You got a camo room and then you wore camo and no one would be able to see you very well in the room. I remember looking at the catalog and thinking, okay, I think I've got the idea but then the whole idea slipped away again. What would you do in the room once you were sort of invisible? I knew from Carl's jokes about married people and beds that there was some kind of business we didn't talk about that went on there, so I thought that must be it. After that, every time I saw someone in camo, I was pretty sure I could locate the activity, anyway.

Then I saw, one right after each other: a young kid in camo, orange and black camo, mossy oak breakup like a bunch of woods paintings, and then the black and white hooded camo. I was sure I was in over my head in the whole business. I was sure I couldn't make sense out of all that. I was sure that neither Carl nor Ben would get me out of this. So I decided that there was some kind of mystery about camo that I would never get no matter how long I tried. Like three-in-one oil. Like Salome's letting me off from the pen-wrecking for a bunch of old papers. Like lots of things in church especially the holy trinity. Like what Ben did and where he went when he didn't have to take me along. Like the magic of D'Angelo's meatball sandwiches.

One time I talked so much about the meatball sandwiches that Salome and mother tried to make some for dinner. Fake meatball sandwiches, Carl immediately said and began poking at his with a knife. I tried mine because the sauce looked okay, but it wasn't even close to okay. I don't know what they did to it but the sauce was bitter, like unhappy. I wanted to put some brown sugar on mine like we did on oatmeal, but Salome said I couldn't but should just eat what's put in front of me and shut up. I don't know if brown sugar would have fixed it, but I think so. Our family is not

Italian, Salome said. Mother said she thought that Italians had some kind of secret grease that made their food taste so good. She was sure that eating too much of it wasn't good for a person and would eventually make you fat and sick. No one in my family is fat and no one in any of the old pictures is fat either. We are all thin, and all of us in the old pictures look right at the camera. We are Krafts and Wenge. Mother was a Wenge before she married father, and then she got the Kraft look after a while.

I don't know where I fit in. I don't have the Kraft *or* the Wenge face. I looked over the old pictures and didn't find anybody like me, but there were a lot that looked something like Ben and Carl and some of the women looked like Salome, the real old ones especially as if the oldest ones had waited to come out as Salome and run things for us.

When I brought the papers to Salome to trade for my life, at first she thought I was bringing her garbage. You could tell. She carefully held one fragile page up to the light like it stunk. Then another one and then another one, and then she smiled.

Thorne

All the children are taken into captivity, the gates are desolate and a multitude of transgressions issue from the cities. All beauty is departed.

As far as I can tell these lamentations came to me earlier than was either good for me or those around me. And when I found the sinking feeling of divorce, when Jane died, when I witnessed my colleagues see-sawing without wit and I wanted to biblically rend my garments and take up sackcloth and . . .

But I wax overly dramatic and out of context. My way is not the way of drama, and it is the way of context. Context is where I find solace and proportion and harmony—the home of the formal beauties of literature. It is where fair and beautiful meet.

Before I met Jane I was expecting her. The page of the manuscript of *Moby-Dick* came trailing clouds of glory. I remember seeing it for the first time, and having eyed the bearer, Godalming, I suddenly was overcome by a piece of paper—very old paper— that carried me away. From Godalming, from Newport, from even my own inner sanctum sanctorum. I had seen holograph versions of Melville's texts before, and letters, and bills of lading, and even notes from the Custom House. The pages weren't numbered, but I recognized immediately where in the book I was reading. Someone had exercised his *sortes vergiliana* to divine which page would come to me so I could stand there struck dumb in front of awesome art, its apotheosis.

The third mate was Flask, a native of Tilsbury, in Martha's Vineyard. A short, stout ruddy young fellow, very pugnacious concerning whales, who somehow seemed to think that the great Leviathans had personally and hereditarily affronted him; and therefore it was a sort of point of honor with him, to destroy them whenever encountered. So utterly lost was he to all sense of reverence for the many marvels of their majestic bulk and mystic ways; and so dead to anything like an apprehension of any possible danger from encountering them; that in his poor opinion, the wondrous whale was but a species of magnified mouse, or at least water-rat, requiring only a little circumvention and some small application of time and trouble in order to kill and boil. This ignorant, unconscious fearlessness of his made him a little waggish in the matter of whales; he followed these fish for the fun of it; and a three years' voyage round Cape Horn was only a jolly joke that lasted that length of time.

Oh joy, I almost said. Oh rapture and excelsior. What I actually said was some hybrid of hum and a grunt—professional skepticism and tincture of feigned disinterest. Godalming stood with his tiny hands clasped behind his back. And he rocked on his heels slightly like a twelve-year-old wearing four thousand dollars of clothing. His shoes had tassels of buttery brown. His sport jacket was vented perfectly to accommodate his insignificant derriere.

The shirt appeared to be silk, the tie nearly no tie but a reference to ties, a work of sartorial accommodation that found a color here and a color there from the rest of his ensemble. All this I saw later when the page of Melville's handwriting had released me from its spell. Godalming stood lyrical palette and unpresuming in front of me. I looked up from the page.

"A wise man once defined culture as 'looking up from the trough.'" Godalming said. "I suppose this is my version of that looking up, though I have family who have chosen not to look up at all."

He laughed a kind of cackle that broke off abruptly. He stood before me with his eyes wide open exaggerating the confidence he had shared as if he wanted something more now in exchange. Would I be his friend in the presence of this gift he had brought me? Would I give him something personal to match his indiscretion? I'm not sure of the entire nature of the discord, but I stood there holding Melville's manuscript, Godalming's whining in my ears, and I had never felt so thoroughly conflicted, bound on both sides by animus and disjuncture at once.

Maybe I misread him completely, and he had no notion of

cultivating me beyond a fee paid for a service. I never found out. I didn't find out either exactly why he wanted the manuscript, whether a passion for Melvilliana, the possibility of an extraordinary investment, some form of bragging rights in his collector group, or just some (and here shows my increasing failure to believe in the innate goodness of humans) ego-pump to keep inflated his porous little sack of self-esteem.

Now I wish we had had more time so that I could have had more information. Maybe I could have been more generous with, Salome's term, the twerp. And twerp or no he did bring me a holograph page of *Moby-Dick*. And I thought about the irascible Flask chasing whales for the fun of it, chasing them as if they were big mice. What a ride that book is: a crew constituted out of a collection of excesses and exotics, a narration that by turns is a collection of short story, novel, play, morality pageant, and religious ceremony. A narrator capable of ethereally drifting off the ship at night and viewing it from a quarter mile away as a metaphoric inferno, and a ship captain driven insane by Nature itself, and all thrown together and spiced by greed and lust and mysterious loomings of satanic figures from the world's great religions. Hell of a book and widely available for under two dollars at any used bookstore. Penny for penny more weird humanity per page than any novel ever written.

The last I saw of Godalming—I assume it was Godalming—was a black body bag being hauled into a police wagon on the dock. Albert had filmed the removal of the body for the police archives, and I, as his former teacher, was given the privilege of a viewing. The light off the harbor water was strong though it was morning light. The Porta-Potty was marine blue with two blue sides, two white sides and top. All Godalming's money couldn't get him any more refined a removal than black plastic and the unceremonial lugging of his guts to the paddy wagon. He probably left the earth with the wafting of the deodorant cake gods, a kind of Wagnerian removal with irony. Oddly, it occurred to me at the moment of the viewing that the Irish had eaten all their elk hundreds of years ago, eaten them to extinction, smacking their lips over the last carcass. I don't know why this occurred to me.

I walked down the hill toward the harbor and the jetty. Clouds stood offshore in a perfect row as if held from the land by an unseen hand. Gulls conspired with the incoming tide, dipping to check out what was to eat from the great store. The charter boats were long gone and five miles out. But a sloop played across the harbor back and forth to get the feel of turns like a child with new roller skates.

I reached the first lumps of the jetty where sand and rock mixed like a shattered Stonehenge strewn toward the water. Part of me just wanted to hand this thing over to other people to work out. Let them cut throats and kiss ass and hustle each other until it's all settled hash. Then someone could copyright the damn thing for all I care and charge a fee online to see it. The manuscript solves a lot of problems. That's why it's interesting at all. It just solves a lot of textual problems.

I was taking the impersonal world personally—shades of Ahab. And like Ahab, there's only so much goddamned coincidence a man can absorb without throwing some kind of perverse punch back, even if it's nothing more than trying to clear the air. After the death of my but-slightly-known Jane, I felt the pull of the monk's cowl even harder; I could go back into that slick darkness of self with the fortress of books around me and never come out. Melville gives us no indication that Ahab had any inkling to retreat from the world, rub his stump and curse at the gods. I had even worked out the calculus of retreat, and had it not been for the recurrence of certain persistent facts, I would have declared defeat and disappeared.

Arvin

I knew I had something with the old papers from the wall because of the reactions of Salome and mother. It took me a long time to figure out that they were quietly excited about having the papers, the part I had given them, anyway. I could catch them whispering to each other, and they'd stop if Ben or Carl or me came into the room. I knew it was the papers but didn't really know what *about* the papers until I crawled up into the wall one afternoon and heard Salome on the phone. We had a phone nook carved out of the plaster wall. From the inside it looked like someone had shaved away all the plaster and replaced it with wall board. I think it must have been changed after the house was built because the phone nook was a place I'd go to because I could hear much better there because the wall was thinner and the nook was between the living room and the dining room, and I could hear both places. So the nook was like a telephone itself, I guess.

Salome was talking to someone about how much money the papers could be worth. "Really?" she said. And, "I wouldn't have guessed that." So I began to think that the papers I didn't give her—way more than half the stack—might be worth something too. I had been saving them out to buy Salome off again in case I did something like I did with her pen.

When I came out of the wall I was careful to dust off completely so I didn't look like a ghost. Salome's hair looked like it did sometimes when she went out in the rain without that plastic babushka with the colored dots on it. Her hair would poof out like it was electric or something. And it always made her eyes look so big and mean like a wolf or a bear.

But she wasn't wet. And she was smiling, and that was even stranger than her hair. She was sweating and smiling. She didn't see me. She said to herself, "Goddamn. Goddamn," which I would be smacked for saying, like when I learned fuckin-A from Carl and tried it out in the backyard thinking I was by myself. Fuckin-A, fuckin-A I said to the bushes. It rang off the garage, and I thought it was so sweet to hold the A like this: AAAAAAAAAA and then bring my hand up in a fist. I got smacked for that by Salome, and she knuckled me on the head.

I thought of my family as animals a lot. Ben was kind of a penguin because he walked stiff and always seemed to be looking off somewhere else, like a penguin. Carl was a small dog for me for a while, one of those biting pointy-nose ones. But later I thought of him as a kind of rat, though I had only seen rats on TV and also one day in Boston when one came out of a sewer toward us and fought with a cat that came out of nowhere. Nobody won. But I thought for a long time that rats could come out of any sewer any time. I expected another one to come, then another one and another. I waited. But that was the only one that did. Mother was a horse. Salome a cobra. I was glad to learn that there were no real cobras in Massachusetts except in the zoo even though Carl said that some had got away from the zoo and nobody knew where they'd gone, and they could be almost anywhere now and making babies. That was Carl's way. I learned not to be too upset by Carl any more than rats.

The only place I could get completely away from all of them was in the walls. Besides the old papers, I kept in the walls on a little shelf I jammed between two studs, small figures I found on the street, plastic soldiers or something but you had to look very close and even then it was hard to make out what they were doing. They were all a dull green before I painted them: one blue, one white, one yellow and one red. I used the paint we had in the basement. The paint that was easy to get off your hands if you spilled, just use water. Then I kept them on the shelf so I could look at them with the flashlight, and they made shadows on the plaster that had squished through. I wondered why the shadows were all the same colors even though the people weren't. Then I saw that maybe the shadows weren't all the same color if you looked at them a long time. On the shelf I also kept a pocketknife I found with one broken blade. Carl and Ben both had pocketknives, but I couldn't have one after I cut myself so bad that one time. So the one I found I kept there on the shelf. Also there was a metal thing; I wasn't sure what it was. But there were five different parts that screwed together different ways and maybe it was a piece of plumbing of some kind. It was brass. I could take it apart and put it back together—the ring part on the tube part and then other square part on the other end of the tube and the other two pieces on that. The best thing of it was just sitting there with the painted people making shadows on the inside of the wall. Oh, and that nobody knew it was there even though it was all right there on the other side of the wall.

Sometimes I'd stand in the living room near where I thought my shelf was and just stand there. Carl said I was just being weird on purpose and that I was "making no effort" to be anything but weird, and that was what was really wrong with me. But standing on the other side of the wall from my painted people and the brass thing made me feel like I had as many secrets from my family as they had from me. And each time I put the brass thing together a different way and changed the people around, then I thought I had another thing they didn't know about. I left the knife with the good blade open and the broken blade inside.

When I lost the privilege of having a pocketknife because I ended up in the emergency room, when Ben or Carl ate most of my meatball sandwich, when Salome only had to point to the sink where the garbage disposer was, and when mother sighed like that when she looked at me, when rats and snakes and horses and penguins made this place a zoo, then I could go to the old papers.

I learned to read them slow, slow, like a spider goes up. I wished I could read like a spider comes down. The papers smelled exactly the same as the walls. I think they had been there so long that they couldn't smell like anything else. I broke a couple of the pages right off before I learned to handle them like Christmas tree

ornaments. I broke a few ornaments before I learned how thin
the glass could be, how mad Ben could get if I broke his favorite
ones. Sometimes just handling the papers carefully made me very
sleepy. I concentrated so hard that I just wanted to fall over and
sleep holding the papers. I knew they were very important for me,
more important than maybe my family, but I wasn't sure how. I
knew because Salome could be so changed by them. The papers
seemed to hoist her up by the scruff of the neck like she used to do
to me, and then carry her off. There was no way I would ever hoist
her up myself in my lifetime. But the papers surely could.

When I was little I remember being with chickens somewhere,
and I can remember also coming to feel more and more like a chicken
the longer they left me with them. I moved like a chicken, pecked
and bobbed my head. I can remember falling into being a chicken
further and further and finding it more and more comforting if Ben
and Carl would just let me be, let me finish becoming a chicken.
They were brown, the chickens, all girl chickens. The people said
the rooster was somewhere else and that he just wanted to attack
whoever came into his hen yard. But he was locked away. They
talked about him kind of hushed as if maybe he'd break out and
come get us all like a rhinoceros. When I had the papers I'd saved
for myself, sometimes I felt like a rhinoceros or maybe just like that
rooster.

I thought of the papers as a secret. Carl told me I couldn't keep
a secret and that was why he and Ben didn't tell me any of theirs.
When I was small I did tell when Salome made me. But I learned
not to. Carl never learned that I learned, but Ben did eventually.
So now that I had a secret I felt so full of the secret sometimes that
I wanted to explode all over Massachusetts. But I never did.

The professor came and went from our house. What Salome
said about the papers she had, I was also saying about the papers I
had. I echoed her. I almost broke out laughing and had to scrootch
down to keep from giggling that day at the table. The professor
seemed okay but Salome was all over his lunch—Carl taught me

to say that. That one dog was all over that other dog's lunch in the fight.

We took a vacation together as a family a long time ago before all the people in the walls said we had no money. Father was already dead and mother said we'd all go to Niagara Falls where he and mother had wanted to go but didn't because Salome came to live with them. She never said where Salome came from, and I only asked once, and mother gave me the sad-eyed look that meant I needed to stop asking or I'd also get the big sigh. And after the big sigh came, I think, a poke in the eye with a sharp stick. Carl said his friend's birthday party was better than a poke in the eye with a sharp stick. Carl taught me lots of things.

Salome was walking around the house smug. She stopped at the mirror in the hall to look at herself. I'd never seen that before. She fluffed her hair on both sides and then bounced down the hall toward the kitchen. She was humming too, and swaying when she walked like the sister of Bill down the street who always walked like that, swayed everyday along in front of our house like the wind was blowing her this way and that.

Salome humming in our house and the papers were why. Sometimes I thought of her not as a cobra but as something I forgot. When I forgot things—the answers in school or what I was supposed to do after I did one thing or to put a belt on my pants (Salome made it a twenty-five cent fine for Ben and Carl and me not to wear a belt. I never paid because I never had the money for it)—it was like what I forgot was a soft thing that I couldn't quite see, but it was there waiting for me to remember it and make it seeable. And when Salome was humming like that, I could almost see what I forgot, but it was too far away or something else maybe, something like too far away.

Thorne

The curse on the manuscript kicked in like a doctrine of eternal return; one rumor of a curse begat a larger rumor begat another. And each rumor had at its heart the previous incarnation, something alike with something different wrapped around the outside as illusion. The press through Porter got ahold of, first, the manuscript and admitted it (they) didn't know the manuscript had been missing and so what? And second, the idea of a curse on the manuscript was much more interesting than any manuscript itself. So whoever touches the manuscript suffers some . . . or whoever just looks at the manuscript . . . or are rays produced that . . . ?

Porter got into the saddle and rode the thing into the sunset and the wire services picked it up. I wondered if Albert had been complicit with the fabrication. Anyway, Porter thought that since the manuscript for *Moby-Dick* contained what he called the *literary essence* of the great book itself, even more *essential* than first editions or autographed copies since Melville personally had adjusted the meaning on almost every page (Porter had not actually seen the manuscript, but was guessing that maybe Melville had done the adjusting), why then whatever mojo (his term) the greatest American novel had, that very mojo was compounded by the number of touches of Melville's hand. However attractive this theory had begun, it now stumbled into half séance, half religious ceremony. He continued that because *Moby-Dick* had such profound presence in American culture and in American ideology — social, political, economic, religious, race/class/gender — why the very paper and ink *contained* the essence of those categories. And citing Hegel's *Aesthetics* and the idea that a literary character contained more authenticity about the culture that it arose from than did the *actual* person on which that character might be based, then Ahab or Ishmael or Queequeg possessed that authenticity and conveyed it to the paper and ink of their creation. Here the jump becomes more gaseous as he argued that curses based on disturbing resting places (Shakespeare, King Tut, The Hope Diamond, etc.) all were based on the assumptions that things at rest wanted to remain at rest—that is, hidden, occult, cryptic—because it was from the hidden state they derived their power and their power to curse. Porter argued from the vested power of the hidden to the logic of people dying from coming in contact with the artifact and finished with a flurry of known curses and historical infelicities that might have been curses and finally the potency of just plain bad luck.

I read Porter fascinated at what the logic of my discipline had wrought. Rhetoric soared and burrowed, lambasted and connived. I came to think of the article later as "Porter's Song." Later, when derivative versions of the song dribbled out of the news services and his original inspired invention (and I suspected a pair of afternoon martinis) had yielded to simpler versions of the MD enterprise, I grew nostalgic for Porter's original epiphany. There was something about the mystical version that got at the eventualities of the whole thing. Especially bad luck. Talk about theory: sin, karma, divine retribution, got-what-he-deserved— no under-theorizing here. Got-what-she-deserved? Jane's unholy broken neck: how had she offended the world so? Job's boils.

I flew back to Oregon baffled by Salome's proposition. I got off the plane in Portland fully resolved to extricate myself completely and wait out the whole acquisitiveness and exercise my scholar's prerogative to eventual access to everything at no personal cost. Let other people bloody their noses.

No personal cost. That was a mistake, I know now.

Jane was a heretic in the old-fashioned sense. According to her story, she came out of Indiana—and in her neighborhood that alone was the first heresy—and joined a group of young men at the Wharton School with voracious appetites for accumulating wealth—second, gendered heresy. And then she graduated and, heresy of heresies, didn't follow her MBA to where the money was, but rather to where the intrigue was. Jane, the heretic adventurer, I came to call her. Jane my cosmic lover. Jane the illusory.

She seemed to embody the shapes of the world, an angle here, a curve there until the geometry coalesced and formed her discipline. Jane was also a hustler in that she was always (it turned out) withholding some information in favor of other information that would create an advantage for her. Her narrated life was, alas, ultimately unreliable, and her invention always outstripped her ethical limitations. In short, I saw her come into my life exactly as I would encounter a charming character in a novel. I committed to her truths no more or less than I did Madame Bovary, or Captain Ahab. I had to say yes to her just long enough for her to gain fictional power in conjunction with my own life. We shared the manuscript of *Moby-Dick* only in the abstract as if it were a plot device to bring us together. There was no real paper involved, just the story of paper.

All this I told myself. And told myself. She was a geometry, and a fictional character.

Here my less literary self whispers, "Fuck you." At least I hear someone whisper that here. "Fuck you," it says, "and furthermore, by what spreading of the legs do you gauge all this, *any* of this, independent of your night at her hotel with too much scotch?" And that's why I try not to listen to that smarmy little turd of a self and his rub-my-nose-in-reality habit. My commitment to the literary always had better leverage in my life since I beat up Earl in sixth grade when he tied to defraud me of my rightful winnings in a marble game. I fought with right on my side; he capitulated with fraud in his nostrils. I finished by kneeling on his arms and pretending to hit him in the face, and then letting him up. Whoever said that violence didn't solve anything was full of shit. Violence solves all kinds of things every day all over the world.

Jane on one side of my story, and Salome on the other. But the real violence was DaGamma. Salome let out—no, it was her mother—that the Kraft family was deeply in debt to someone who sold the debt to someone else who either was DaGamma or

DaGamma got it from them.

Salome: "No it was my mother."

Caroline (in Seattle): "My family has a debt that we cannot repay immediately, and we want the manuscript to free us from this obligation and then use the remainder to finance our company more securely." The debt was to DaGamma, but just how severe the debt was, how urgent the need for repayment—these weren't clear because I didn't know what questions to ask. I was still full of the flush of having been reluctantly drawn back into the world by Albert and his Seattle cohorts.

Somebody owes somebody else a bunch of money and you step into the buzz saw looking for a scab. Why on this planet would you choose that if you had to choose between fishing and that? I'm not sure why people forget this, you can always go fishing instead of the thousand foolish things you're thinking of doing, flying up people's noses. It had the rhythms of an Irish sermon.

I looked for what could be called the phosphorescence of any situation.

I will assemble everyone here, though they never assembled themselves, in order to give them all an opportunity to make for me some sense of this.

Salome: "What the problem is, Doctor Thorne, is that the manuscript grows in value while we speak. And every wire service that picks up the story adds to our eventual windfall. We *own* that manuscript, my family, in the full philosophical sense of what that word means. We have outlived our bad luck and are coming into good luck. That's what it means to us. We have mixed our bad-luck labor with it in the Lockean sense and now own it."

Enter Porter and Salome turns to him. "I hope you're not with the press."

"As a matter of fact I am, and I make no attempt to hide it. I understand that you—your people—are the responsible parties when it comes to the Melville manuscript. And I'd like to ask you a few questions."

I bet you do, I would add under my breath. Salome holds her nose theatrically and turns away from Porter. Does she make an appliance reference?

Arvin takes her place. He looks at Porter curiously. He's never spoken to a reporter before and doesn't quite know where to start. Potter beats him to it.

"So you're the brother? You found the manuscript? Tell me about how that happened."

My version of Arvin says that he was just in the right place at the right time. That the whole business was felicitous as if the manuscript had waited for the propitious moment to come to light. The real Arvin probably just affected the Arvin-stare used for people outside the Kraft family: brows scrunched, head slightly turned to give the effect of looking at you askance, one earlobe tugged repeatedly.

But Porter wants his interview. He says, "What do you think of your sister, Arvin? What did she say when you gave her the papers the first time?"

"Nothing," says he.

"Well. Then did you know how valuable they were when you saw them? Was it like finding money?"

"It was like finding meatball sandwiches. It was like finding plover's eggs and sand dollars and cents. It was cashing in."

Salome wants to return here to the talk of money but instead Ben and Carl come in and flank Arvin, a little too close, making a sandwich of their brother. Caroline watches closely her trinity of sons.

"Herman Melville was a writer of sea stories," said Ben seriously.

"He was a New Englander though really from New York City." Carl put his arm around Arvin's shoulder. "He published *Moby-Dick* in 1851."

They exit, taking Arvin whom Porter believed was about to spill the beans, whatever beans there were. He suspected beans. Porter takes another crack at Salome. Gene Anczyski appears but stands like a ghost who's trying to think of something to say. Salome waves him off with the back of her hand, and he fades. Salome is explaining to Porter the difference between D'Angelo's meatball sandwiches and DaGamma lending group. Mrs. Kraft is walking in tighter and tighter circles.

I've been sitting on this bench on the dock breathing in diesel fumes from the *Cisco-Marie*, a rust-bucket trawler, and the engine is running near wide open to test something, pumps maybe since she's shooting water ten feet straight out her side. I was imagining the tale's principle characters all gathered on the stage of my mind with number two diesel blowing in through the ventilation ducts. The audience, silent but respectful. I was getting a headache from the stink. Jane was scheduled to appear, I think, but never did. Maybe like Godalming—also a no-show. Maybe because they were dead.

A young man came down the dock carrying a squid in one hand. He had the appearance of someone looking for a place to cook his capture. The squid hung nearly to the dock, and he had trouble keeping it from dragging. He continued past me without a word, and I found myself wishing he'd join the group coalesced around my headache. The play could use a dead squid and a handsome young sailor. But no luck. He floated by and onto shore where sailors are sailors no more but beached entities waiting for an outgoing tide.

Then Gene figures he has something to say and begins a peroration complete with gestures about whales and what they do on the surface of the ocean. Gene wants the assembled to know what a hell of a book this thing is. The whale sounds. Gene nods at the whale sounding, a huge Polish hand heading for the bottom of the sea. All are bathed in the light of a headache.

Arvin

Ben once made a trap for the paperboy who Salome told not to walk across the lawn, but always did anyway and made a path. The first version had nails in a board buried just under the grass so the nails would poke up when he stepped there. But when Salome saw it she said he couldn't. The next version had black fishing line tied back and forth to trip him, but he could easily see it and walked around. Salome made Ben take down the fishing line because she said it was unsightly she said, like junk. Ben gave up and Carl took over.

Carl made a kind of trap that let the paperboy walk all the way across the yard and then just before he got to the neighbor's then there was a trigger that set off a thing that shot ketchup at his pants and splattered him from the knees down. Salome approved this fake blood, Carl called it, because no one was going to get hurt or sued. But the paperboy's mother called our mother and asked if we were some collection of mental patients that would do that to her son, and she had to use lye soap to get out the stains and it ruined the cloth too. There had always been some kids in the neighborhood that couldn't play with us. Carl told me it was because of me. Ben said it was because of Salome that we had problems with our neighbors. Mother kept going around being nice to people, but once when she took a casserole to someone who had someone die in their family, they said no thank you. Mother cried. Salome said nothing but marched off to her room and didn't come down until dinner. I was always trying to figure these things out, the things that other people seemed to get right away. The casserole thing that made Mother cry was harder than most, but I didn't give up. So then finally I could see that those people thought the food was poison or something, maybe not clean food or it was trick food like rubber vomit. Carl said it was because we lived twenty-five years behind everyone else in the neighborhood, and they didn't trust us because we were time travelers. I gave up on Carl. But I did see why they sent the food back.

The papers I found in the wall were what was going to make us okay with everyone. There would be money and that would be everything. Sometimes I could go into the walls, up the dumbwaiter shaft (Carl called me the dumbwaiter sometimes, but Salome made him stop, so he never called me it then where she could hear, and he knew I didn't tattle for stuff like that—for anything). The only light was from the basement window that scattered up there a short ways. After that I could see light looking down but not up. The light was like in church. But I think what I liked best being inside the wall, better than being able to hear secretly, better than Salome and Carl not being able to find me, was that nobody in Massachusetts even suspected I was here and so I was completely alone.

Salome talked to someone on the phone. I did the putting together while in the walls where it was quiet, and I could find out how the parts came together. At first it seemed like one of Carl's machines that he made out of things he found in the garage— washing machine pieces, rope, old blinds. At first only Carl could see how the things went with each other, and he'd go to work. He'd hook this to that and those to something else and then finally the pieces to the pieces and the thing would work. It would raise or lower something. Once he made a thing for a parade float for the high school, and it was supposed to wave a big arm of Paul Bunyan, and it did. That's how I got to understand what was going on with Salome and the guy on the phone. The other guy on the phone was Professor Rhinoceros.

So the one guy had lent Salome money with the papers as a kind of hostage. I had to be the hostage four times with Carl being the kidnapper, so I knew about hostages—duct tape and all. And the professor was an expert on the papers. I finally figured out that I wanted to be on the side of the expert since I had more than half of the papers, and he'd be a better friend to have. Ben was the one who would talk to me about choosing my friends and how I should look for allies in case of trouble. Really though, I took anyone who wasn't mean to me in the neighborhood, and they were mostly girls who I think felt sorry for me.

So I choose the professor because I knew that I'd need an ally if my plan was going to work out. There were meatball sandwiches in it, you bet. But it was more than meatball sandwiches that made this machine go. But every time I thought of my brothers and summer and meatballs, I got madder. And when I got mad, I wasn't so good at thinking like when I wasn't.

The time had come for me to separate from my family. At first just the idea of living on my own seemed impossible because I wasn't earning any money. But money seemed to be the only problem. And when I found the papers and found that they were a kind of money for Salome, then I thought I could spend them myself. Then I found it didn't cost very much to live in Mexico. Then I found they had meatballs in Mexico and called them *albondigas*. All this took a while, but it was Professor Thorne that made it work. He called me, I think to talk to Salome, but we talked instead.

Every time I said his name, Professor Thorne, I pictured Carl with that rose thorn glued to his nose. I couldn't help it. Professor Thorne and Carl's endless shenanigans, that's what Salome called Carl's fooling around, endless shenanigans, got mixed together in my head just like in school sometimes when the teacher had changed the subject from social studies to math, but I was still doing social studies when the math story problem came up, and I was wondering why when Tom was twice as tall as his sister but half as tall as his father, nobody could ask Tom or his sister or his father anything suddenly. But a couple minutes ago there was lots more information about somebody and his sister and his father, and people could talk to the family and did and found out all kinds of things including how tall they were. I wasn't anybody's fool but sometimes I felt like my own.

It rained and rained that afternoon. I sat on the window seat watching the way the rain made little circles in the puddles when it hit. I was thinking I should hear a plop, but there were so many little circles that all the plops ran together. I felt like that one time when we went to New York City, and I tried hard to listen to all the people around but couldn't hear any one of them. Anyway, I was just staring out the window trying to find my way into the rain the way I would when I was younger. Now I can't even remember it very well, but I could watch the rain and then suddenly feel like I wasn't watching at all but was the rain, like there was no difference between me and the rain. Somehow I lost how I could do that, and it made me feel sad and try harder. But the harder I tried, the more I couldn't, like it was the trying that made it impossible.

It rained and Salome, Ben and Carl were at work doing construction things. Mother was what she called "tucked up" on the couch in the other room sewing something with a blanket over her legs and her feet up. It rained straight down and made the grass light up green. Robins were working in the rain and seemed to get worm after worm without so much as a hop between. I gave up on getting all the way into the rain and instead the robins were telling me something I could almost get but couldn't. There was thunder far away. I always thought thunder came from New York City—probably something Carl told me—so I was thinking about New York and the time we went. Somewhere between the robins and New York City I realized I could leave and take the papers with me like they were money and then, I don't know, lots of things would fall into place that hadn't before.

Too many things had happened that were awful. Lamentable. Oh, that's so lamentable, Ben would say. You're lamentable, Carl shot back. You're the lamest lamentable. Once when I said I'd stop them from picking on me when I got as old as they were, Carl pointed out to me that I would never be as old as they were— ever. They would always be older and so nothing would ever change from the way it was. He drew a picture, well, a line, that had numbers on it and showed me how with each of my birthdays they'd both have a birthday, too. This is it, Carl said. The way it is, is the way it will always be, and I thought that settled it until I found the papers and sat with them until they seemed to breathe — in and out, in and out. Maybe it was my own breathing I heard, but I could hear it suddenly and I couldn't before. I could make the way it would be different.

And Carl and Ben and mother and Salome couldn't do anything about it if I did the business right. Not too long ago I would never get the idea to do this all by myself. Finding the papers and saving my life from the disposer with part of them and then visiting the papers nearly every day. I think that was it, that's what did it for me. I don't think the painted soldiers or the knife or the brass pieces had anything to do with it. Okay, so maybe the brass pieces did. A joke. I *know* it was the papers and even how they did it for me.

I remember looking at the papers the first time and thinking I was seeing drawings, not words. Carl used to draw maps with tiny letters on them. So tiny they looked like lines that were drawing something. He wrote in spirals out from the center and had to keep turning the paper as he wrote. I tried to write like this once but couldn't because I'd forget to turn the paper enough to make the spiral work. But Carl could sit all afternoon by himself and make drawings with tiny words. Ben did things too but different things. Ben would make drawings of things like a nut and bolt except you could sort of see through both and how they went together with the threads. And trickier things too. Drafting he said it was. I didn't even try these because I couldn't see through things like he could. They were my brothers, but I couldn't do what they could, and before I found the papers that bothered me. It was like we didn't have the same mother or father, like maybe I came from someplace else and came to live with these people. I asked mother about why I was different and did I come from somewhere else than they did and she said, "We all come from God," as if that explained everything. Salome walked past and mother sighed so long that I thought she might use up all the air in the room with her sigh. We both watched Salome walk down the hallway and out of sight. I thought that maybe Salome had something to do with why I was different from Ben and Carl. Sometimes I felt as if Salome had leaned over me, maybe while I was sleeping, maybe I was a baby, and sucked all the quickness out of me, maybe licked it off of me like a cat licks milk off your finger. I wasn't sure exactly what Salome had to do with me, so I decided that she wasn't my real sister. I even tried this out on mother, starting with Salome and thinking I'd go on to Ben and Carl after a while. Mother looked at me a long time and asked now why would I ask a thing like that, and what would she be if she wasn't my sister.

I don't know why I said it. It just came out and there it was, and I don't know why because I didn't think even for second and there it was. I said Salome was my mother.

I might have said the f-word or something else that mother didn't allow — ever. She said a lot of things after that but she never said that Salome wasn't my mother. So I thought that if Salome was my mother then that would explain why she was so . . . the way she was, and I was so the way I was. She used up all the fast and left me with the slow. But that could mean she didn't have any slow — that I had it all.

Thorne

Albert let me see the police report that related in that eviscerated language—in which people become individuals—exactly how Jane was found. I read the prose like literature for its nuance and image patterns and found her sitting behind the wheel with her eyes closed, head off to the right side like a sleeper waiting out the witch's curse to awake in a better, more princely time. These times of constantly peering back over the shoulder, this angst and backpedaling and furtive glancing crap, a fine young woman could wait out this stuff asleep behind the wheel in a cow pasture with Holsteins and spring grass lavished like the grace of God across the coastal landscape. Turn the police page. Her feet had lost their shoes upon impact, but both shoes were there on the driver's side. She wore a blue sweater, light blue the report said but I knew it was sky blue like one of those summer days when the clouds sat far offshore and the water skittered out to the sky swapping color back and forth until the sky ate up everything into sky blue. That was the sweater she was wearing when she left. She must have taken off her coat to drive, but she had left it on most of the time we were outside, even for the first ten minutes in the restaurant until she got warm enough. She might have been always on the edge of being cold that weekend: her toes were cold in bed, her nose was cold touching just below my ear, the tips of her fingers stayed cool under every condition of feeling and touching. I think her Indiana childhood with its winters that could cover the neighbor's junk . . . I think she was . . . I think she knew she was in over her head for the first time.

She had said that the people she worked for, represented, always wanted passionately what they wanted. And in the past they had been willing to cover all contingencies with enough money to make happen exactly what they wanted to happen. They were phone numbers and fax numbers to her. She was expected to check in regularly and prosecute their interests.

The day she died in the pasture, bucolic death in the pastoral tradition, she had clear weather that should have meant clear sailing in the maritime tradition. A light ground fog in the morning burned off and dispersed inland around ten followed by an onshore breeze just enough to mess her hair. She had held it to the side and kissed me. "That's not business," she said. "That's just a kiss. And here's another one." The light blue sweater was just visible sticking out the top of her coat. The wind freshened by afternoon but not enough to blow a car off the highway. I never rode anywhere in her car with her and didn't know if she was a good driver or not. Did she use her turn signal always? Did she check her blind spot before pulling into the next lane? Jane that weekend sometimes made it hard for me to breathe. The police report said her neck appeared broken when they found her with no other obvious signs of trauma. She put on her brakes because there were skid marks on the road; the brakes seemed to have worked. The undercarriage of the car was packed with the soft soil and grass of the pasture, and it appeared that the vehicle dropped some eight feet from the roadway to the pasture and continued through the electric fence coming to rest sky blue and peacefully facing the grazing herd.

I returned the police report to Albert and asked him if he had written it. He said he had re-written it from the officer's notes, and then the officer who found her had initialed his version. That particular officer, Albert said, always had difficulty getting the reports written up so the Chief had come up with a system in which he could sign off on others having written the report for him. Otherwise he was an exemplary officer, punctual and conscientious. So Jane had been found by the least literate officer on the Newport force, and I got her tale secondhand.

"The appalling ocean surrounds the verdant land," Melville wrote. I got the feeling for the appalling at the level of my seasickness, but that's not what he meant. The appalling part was its magnificent indifference to human conduct. Jane's death, the two men walking on the street, I began to figure them both equal. "It's just a kiss." It's just her neck. It's just a store full of whale kitsch—whales hanging from monofilament line, whales in burnished blue metal, crystal whales, whales with baby whales, whales and whales and whales. After Jane, I went beyond the appalling indifference of the ocean to my puny lusting after her. The two men on the street it seemed had some other two men and then other two men, all of whom thought I had something directly to do with the manuscript when at that time I didn't. A week after Jane's death I went hiking on Cape Foulweather and that was where I met more of the walking men and had my hands shredded, something that never happens in the scholar's world.

* * *

Arvin and I became allies through a complicated, strange set of circumstances that started with my phone call to him, well really to his mother, but I ended up talking to him about the family business. He had enough of an idea about his family's financial straits to spill the beans. His words. He said he'd spill the beans to me because the beans needed spilling, and he lived almost in Boston and everyone knew about Boston and beans. Then that cackle of his to let me know I was in the presence of a joke. Talking to Arvin–and the phone seemed to make this even more evident: the remove, the electronics of the call, the second-degree distance, the whole over-thereness of it—was like speaking one language but hearing the answer from a translator. Things could mean this or that; it was simple but had a complicated aura to it. I'd ask him how the family was, how the business was working out, and he'd say that Carl was taking a course but he didn't know what, that Ben bought a harmonica, that his mother seemed quiet and Salome hated carrot soup. He framed almost every answer radiating out from himself in the same order: Carl, Ben, mother, Salome, as if that order contained all the connections he needed. I kept casting about for a literary character to compare him to but found only fragments and pieces: not a Benjy or Darl from Faulkner, not a Billy Budd from Melville. He came on again through the phone. I had asked if the manuscript—I used "papers" since he had—was in a safe place and protected from the weather. His answer made me realize for the first time that there were either two manuscripts or Arvin just wasn't a good source for information.

"Carl, he's the one who finds out everything. He gives Indian burns and Dutch rubs and little hugs and snakebites. The one I hate the most is snakebites. Then I hate little hugs because they're really just pinches. Ben doesn't care. He's like mother that way. Both of them just look at the walls sometimes, and you have to ask them something over and over until they answer. Salome doesn't do what Carl does to hurt me. I don't know exactly what she does, but I'm more afraid of her than Carl. The papers are safe enough. As safe as a house. As safe as a bank. Carl doesn't like tight places. Ben doesn't like spiders. And the soldiers are guarding and guarding too. Once we had two meatball sandwiches to split, and I got almost nothing. I remember. Carl and Ben took most. Salome wanted a bite. When it got to me I could hold it in my fingertips. Almost nothing. When Salome touched it with her lips I almost didn't want it at all. They never let me have a fair share. The papers are okay. Yup, just okay."

Arvin only needed a little priming, and he ran on wherever it was he directed himself. I left the phone without talking to Mrs. Kraft. I left thinking that I was dealing with the wrong Kraft consortium if I wanted to know where the manuscript was.

I remember one summer when I was ten or eleven and had to buy a black cherry soda and a big, salty pretzel every summer day as if the rotation of the earth depended on it. The summer heat, the sound of wind in the trees, the way my muscles wrapped my bones deliciously were all amplified by the soda and pretzel, piped up and into a dizzying grasp of being alive. Somewhere in there was an Arvin in a permanent state of Huck Finnery but not so wise maybe as Huck Finn. Not so independent, I thought. That was wrong because Arvin turned up in Newport having flown across the country to Portland, taken a bus, then another bus to the coast. He was four days getting to Newport including sleeping in various bus terminals waiting for the next connection. Arvin came to Newport because he said he suddenly could, and he had some news for me and a proposition.

* * *

He arrived on a clear day with my phone number. "This is Arvin," he announced. "This is Arvin, and I'm in Newport, Oregon."

This was triumphant, as if he'd mustered all the ego he could out of the Pacific sea air. I, Arvin, have conquered the great width of the United States of America. I, Arvin, have driven off the enemy hoards and pacified the region. I have slain the beasts, laid waste to scoundrels and . . . I stood looking at Arvin at the bus station. "What have you done?" was what I could think of while looking at him. He had on a hooded sweatshirt with Harvard University across the front and a shield below it—heraldic and crimson, ancient but standing there in front of me like a melted candy on a hot sidewalk. He carried a backpack of Boy Scout green. Off one side was hanging a shred of baby blue ancient blanket pinned to the pack with an enormous safety pin.

Arvin to break your heart. Arvin to sing all the ancient lays. Arvin the surprise and elemental heart-song.

Feed him, I thought. Must feed Arvin because by his own tales of himself, eating was the beginning of all endings with him. I thought hard for us both: where could a person encounter acceptable meatball sandwiches on this coast? I came up empty, and so I decided that spaghetti would have to be the next best thing.

Arvin engaged the spaghetti substitute with gusto. I had

a sandwich and waited for him to make his purposes clear. Small talk with Arvin was not a useful distinction since almost everything said was a version of small talk. He seemed to have a lack of gravity until suddenly the swirl came to mean more by the crashing together of the words, more than the mere order, syntax and grammar. He employed the logic of simultaneity and imperative. The imperative he supplied by peering out of the hood, brown hair sticking beatific in bristles out the sides. The peering was something of a Saint Francis intently waiting for the animals to come out of the woods where he meditated. Arvin, what's on your mind?

The sword, the pen, the sackcloth and ashes—all available to me as a young man. I could have chosen any one. I could not have chosen insurance underwriting or politics or any profession that required me to be on the telephone for any length of time. I have trouble even calling the device a phone, the telephone, as if the short form let the damn thing loose on the world, and had we maintained the tele then it would have stayed at bay. I can talk on telephones; I only hate it: can't see a raised eyebrow, can't hear anger or capitulation to a voice, no smirk or pout or flirt. The telephone is like talking to someone at the other end of long tunnel.

Arvin is a little like that too. Way down there is Arvin and you shout into the opening and wait. Out comes some garbled stuff with just enough information so you can make a good guess what he means. Arvin in Newport carrying his backpack: he's passing along the harbor with me, and he's looking at the boats to read the sterns. I suddenly wonder if he doesn't have the manuscript in the backpack. Then I can't get out of my mind that he has the manuscript in the backpack, the salt air is seeping in and eating the words off the page even as we walk off his spaghetti lunch.

"Body and Soul," he reads. "Port Orford."

"Katie and Me," I point out. "Charleston, Oregon."

Maybe we could come to some arrangement about the papers. I could copy them very carefully and give them back. I'd promise not to gain anything by having them. I'd promise to help him sell them to the Newberry Library or some legitimate collector. For a lot of money.

"Annie Tootle," he laughed. "Newport, Oregon. Tootle. Tootle. Tootle."

Suddenly he could see the whole highway bridge across the outlet to the river, and he stopped: the bridge's great structural MMMs standing against the north and south jetties that reached out to the ocean. And then Arvin did a strange thing. He took my arm like a lady holding on to walk down steps in high-heeled shoes. Gently and then just balanced there looking at the bridge as if it might turn colors or spell out something. We stood there in the coastal afternoon watching into the haze blowing in from the water, and the bridge did seem pendant and ethereal carrying repeatable toy cars that appeared at each end and proceeded against the sky and then disappeared as if only the bridge were real and the land a fake where the vehicles were swallowed whole.

Jane had said on her first day at Newport that everyone seems to squint here. "Don't squint, Charles, or you'll stay that way forever." Don't squint. Don't.

Jane said the light was different here than any other coast she'd been to. I suggested that we were looking west, and that was the reason. West light. Sundown light and the shivering of the sun going in the drink. No, she said. I think it's something else altogether. I think it's because you can't go farther than this. You've run out of west places to get away to, and you have to squint to see if there's something else out there, someplace more to go. She said she thought she'd squint too if she lived here very long. Arvin didn't squint though; his eyes grew large and round and seemed to eat up the bridge from one end to the other and then back again, his hand soft on my arm.

From the vantage of fifteen years ago, the advantage of not knowing yet the dead Jane, the world-weary Dean of students who had greeted my arrival with a laconic wave and a "welcome to the end of the Western world," my wife at my side weakly smiling and sizing up the magnitude of our disaster, the manuscript of *Moby-Dick* safely lost forever, I could not have seen my way to the tableau of Arvin and me and the grey-green Newport bridge in a summer haze. I felt lost in the voyage like any Ishmael.

Arvin said that before he went to my apartment to rest he'd have to contact his family to let them know he was all right. I offered my phone, but he insisted he'd rather go to a public phone and reverse the charges. He insisted I go wait for him at home while he called. And he was off by himself bobbing along in his hood like a Wagnerian troll on vacation at the Oregon coast.

I waited for hours and had begun to think he wouldn't come back when he knocked at my door, came in and asked for a place to nap. He hadn't slept well on the trains and busses and was exhausted. I fixed him the couch and went out to the University to see if anything was interesting in my other life, the life in which there were no trolls, no accidents, no magic manuscripts.

Arvin

I left Mr. Rhinoceros and said I had to call home. But what I really wanted to do was get rid of the papers into a safe place. Once I had tried to keep my cowboy bank from my brothers who knew how to get money out without opening it or breaking it. They used a butter knife. So I carried it everywhere with me until Carl began to call me Jangles. I only had about three dollars in coins in there. I slept with it tucked under my chin, but finally they got it away from me while I was sleeping and took most of the money. They left enough to jangle a little but I could tell most of it was gone. I woke up with my bank under my chin, but they got the money all right. After that, I hid the bank in a high place in the wall where it was guarded by what Ben and Carl were afraid of. I decided to do the same thing with the papers that Salome didn't get, the ones I traded for my life.

When I saw the bridge across the river with the ocean on the other side, I knew I found the place. The bridge looked like giant Ms and then had all kinds of Xs I could climb. I thought there were lots of people who wouldn't like to climb around up there because they'd be afraid to fall. I found out that I wasn't afraid that way one afternoon when I was pretty little, and I climbed to the top of a maple that sat between our yard and our neighbor's. The top of the tree was even with the top of our neighbor's tall house. The tree got skinnier and skinnier as I got to the top until it was a stick in my hands. I wrapped my legs around it like it was a rope. And if I leaned to one side the whole top would bend way over and then slowly bend back up almost straight and then bend the other way. I think I was doing this for a long time when I heard mother down below calling my name. I didn't think she could see me way up there so I pretended I couldn't hear her. Then her voice got different, like she was talking to a baby. She kept saying the same things over and over about how she had something for me, a surprise, that I'd like if I just came down. Then she stopped and Salome's voice came up the tree just like the ants that crawled upside down. Her voice got up to my feet louder and louder and I found myself going back down even if I didn't want to. I didn't know why they wanted me down until mother explained that I could get hurt if the tree broke, and that most people would be afraid the tree would break. I knew the tree wouldn't break, I told them, but I don't know why I knew.

The bridge underneath was like a gigantic jungle gym. There was so much to hold onto once you got up the cement posts near the bottom. That part was easy too. I just leaned a long skinny log against one post and ran up the stick then shimmied up the iron into the jungle gym. It was noisy because of the cars going over, and I could hear the waves, and the higher I got the better I could see the waves and the water. I hid the papers in a safe place wrapped in a garbage bag and duct taped it to one of the Xs. I had everything I needed in my backpack. Then I sat for a while and just looked out. I wanted to remember where I was and what I was here for and what shits Ben and Carl were, especially Carl.

I once showed Carl how I could run up the side of the house for a ways if I got a good running start. I could run up and then turn around and sort of run down. I left footprints on the house, but sometimes I could run up far enough that I could grab the gutter and pull up and then keep going right up the downspout to the roof. So I showed him. He just stood there with his hands on his hips, and I shouted down, "Pretty good, huh?" and he went into the house to get mother to show her the footprints up the side of the house. That was the end of that. Oh, then he started calling me monkey-boy and making sounds. At the dinner table all he had to do was make a little monkey sound kind of under his breath. Then I couldn't eat because he told me that the family got me from the zoo, and they could take me back any time. Any time *he* said. So he made monkey sounds to let me know I would have to go back. I found out I wasn't from the zoo either. And then I learned to flip

Carl off when he did the monkey sound thing. Ben taught me how to do it and not show mother or Salome. I practiced doing it right, the way Ben showed me with the fingers bent with the nails on my palm next to the important finger. Ben said if you don't do it right it doesn't mean anything at all.

Sitting up inside the bridge was very nice. I knew my pirate treasure was safe there. I liked the way the birds flew below and so slow that it looked like I could walk down them like steps, how the wind was like a hand with fingers feeling around in the bridge. Maybe looking for me. I had to scold myself to go down because the professor would be waiting for me, and I didn't want him to see where I'd gone because he'd figure out then where the papers were. When I came down, the wind began to blow, and I knew no one else would go up there just for fun. Monkey boy from the zoo could go, but no one else.

When I got down the water was coming up around the post. I jumped to the dry part but as I watched the water came up around the pole and knocked over my running-up stick. The tide came in same as Boston. I knew the papers would be even safer with the tide in.

The professor took me to his house after he bought me some spaghetti. I think it was the climbing or the spaghetti, but I couldn't wait to go to sleep. It felt like I'd been traveling for a long time even though it was only a few days, and I hadn't slept very much. On the bus I slept wrapped around the papers so no one could steal them. I kept thinking the papers would be so many meatball sandwiches even though I knew they weren't. Then they were doubloons and other pirate treasure. And rubies. Rubies always looked so delicious, and I always wondered what they would taste like. I was wondering that aloud one time and Carl heard and said they would just taste like stones and that the red color wouldn't taste at all. He said emeralds wouldn't taste like anything green either, and then he went into a list of other things that didn't taste like what they looked like they should taste like. He said he read somewhere that snakes tasted like chicken and people tasted like pigs. He didn't ever eat a snake or a person, but he said other people had, and they said that. I thought the snake part I could get along without. But somehow eating people seemed interesting, and I wondered if a person could eat himself or it would have to be somebody else. And so I wondered if you could eat your own toes or maybe just one to start with just to see if you wanted to eat the rest of yourself. That way you could stop any time, but you wouldn't have a toe, of course. My mistake was telling Carl anything, anything at all. He just stood looking at me with his hand on his chin. Then he told me I was being raised by the family as an experiment from Harvard University, and now he could tell them that their experiment had failed. And he walked away and wouldn't even talk to me about eating yourself. He said the experiment used monkeys to do something and then something else and then there was me. He laughed all the time he was telling me, but I wasn't sure what was so funny.

And so I learned the not telling part of what I knew. It seemed the more that I kept to myself — what I thought or wanted or wished for or hated — the more things built up inside like piles of wood, like the wood our neighbor piled up to burn in his woodstove. He stacked sticks of it alongside the house. Ben and Carl dared me to steal some and they'd burn it in our fireplace, so I did. I stole some small sticks and once I stole some after a snowstorm and the neighbor saw the tracks and came to our door. Salome had to apologize to him at the front door, and we three hid because we knew she hated to apologize about anything. She made us all stand in a row in front of her and gave us the talking in her special voice that felt like ice and fire at the same time. I told her that I stole the wood, and she told me how disappointed she was in me that I didn't act like a human being. Carl waited until she was done and then whispered "see" to me and said "Harvard." But he and Ben made me do it in the first place. At first I was happy when Ben went into the construction business because he was gone most of the day. But that left Carl alone to think of things to do to me. And then Carl went into the business, at first a little, then more. Salome sat them down at night to talk to them about how they had done that day. I knew I wouldn't go into the business, and it was one of the things that made me glad. Glad as a meatball sandwich.

Thorne

Gene Anczyski showed up in Newport even before Arvin had. He asked about the *Moby-Dick* manuscript on the phone, and then he appeared like a giant genie in a puff of smoke. I began to think of him as a genie too, because he had the habit of appearing and disappearing that bore little resemblance to the ways regular humans came and went. He said he had investments in northern California that he had to look after. Also he had friends in the investment world that got together regularly to talk about the tides and currents of investments. Most of them were former NBA players who had retired before the immense salaries had appeared and made millionaires out of both the multi-year salary guys and their sports agents. He called his friends the "old guys" and each of them, it seemed, had a specialty investment area to make the most of what money they had earned for bone-crunching services. One did small apartment buildings. One studied modern art, and he presently ruled the investment roost with a 45 percent ten-year average return. Safer though were shopping mall chains starting with cinnamon buns and ranging to sausage franchises and large-women clothing outlets. The key was that everyone shared and let the "old guys" in on whatever seemed a good thing. Gene said that they thought of themselves as a kind of informal consortium that had only a few rules—full disclosure before investment was first, and no recriminations about losses was second. All for one, and everybody takes it in shorts equally when the investment tanks. Gene's area was paper—manuscripts, signed documents, memorabilia and sports photos, especially signed photos from championship teams. The Melville manuscript was new ground but, he claimed, finally not that different in kind from an autographed photo of Mickey Mantle.

Gene's puff of smoke appeared in Newport while I was still trying to parse the death of Jane. Without actually raining the day he came, the air packed in moisture and licked the coastline, and I sat host to Gene's guest, I think in the spirit of still cooperating with the police, maybe in the spirit of finding out who chased me through the salal and shredded my hands. I also thought that it would be good if Gene caught the sons-a-bitches with one of those hands like a Polish ham, though I had no idea how that might happen. We drank beer, and he toasted the weather coming in.

"To the wet and wild coming on shore," he held up a beer.

"Forty-percent chance, says the weatherman."

"Okay, so here's the deal. If you can get the manuscript together, I can assemble enough money to make a serious bid on it. Yeah, yeah, there will be other bids but think of this. If my group buys it, we deliver it to the Newberry Library Melville collection and make a deal with them for a huge tax deduction, and the library makes it available to scholars—online, all the stuff they do. That's how you win. We win by the deal we make with the Newberry. We've been doing very well recently and need to take some of the tax burden off our gains."

I was thinking about Jane's neck snapped in a vanilla rental car, the slumped body of Godalming reeking of deodorant cake, my hamburger hands and then the Krafts and Salome's mouth moving as I peered across my Triscuit at her. Gene's logic was becoming impeccable from a scholar's standpoint. If I had control of the manuscript, his plan seemed reasonable and righteous. What I knew for sure was that a page of it existed, and what I had been told was that there was more, maybe the whole thing with Arvin.

A weariness set in. The art of the deal held no interest for me. You do this; I'll do that. Then other people will jump in and do other things, and we'll aim for satisfaction and legal consequences to non-performance. . . . Even the language made me weary. I had been too long outside the getting and spending to be able to even fake interest in the process. The idea of a curse as a cultural construct—that was interesting. Having the author's intentions for a great American novel—that too. But sitting with Gene and listening to the particulars of museum and library donation customs and like-kind exchange and "consideration" used in a way I'd never considered, well, these left my mind wandering to: the weather again, the accumulated bad luck that seemed packed into this year, the theories of luck different authors spun out of words, words, words.

As Gene talked about the Newberry Library deal, I found myself trying to predict what form of accident might befall a genie, a man who creaked audibly when he stood up, an enthusiast and amateur scholar in the best sense of amateur—a lover of things.

When I came to literature it was more of a fleeing than attraction, though the attraction of words was always a part. The soul's passage here, that's what calls to me–a parable of how holiness creeps into our lives and mixes like water and honey. First the fleeing.

I never minded physical work, only the repetition. Something in doing the same thing over and over exhausted me in the same way that Gene's careful explanation of eleemosynary dealings sent me to pondering the weather. I figured that everybody had to be stupid about something, and that would be my thing. I couldn't find the charm in repetition, and so I fled. First, it was science and the complicated branching of knowledge contained by verifiable experience. Then came words with their potent associations and the whole calculus of poetry, its imaginative largeness, and prose, its elegant structure and human meanings. Melville became my scholarly passion combining the two with the addition of his mad plunge through the second half of the 19th century's love affair with language—theory and practice, philosophy and metaphysics.

I remember in second grade learning from a worldly fellow-student the poem: "Ladies and gentlemen/Take my advice/Pull down your pants/And slide on the ice." I should have known then that language would win out. I thought: how precise, how funny, how unexpected, how far from repetition! Or maybe not exactly that, but I remember being so taken with the poem that I carried it home to my mother like a jewel I had unearthed and spoke it to her proudly. She tolerated it, smiled and seemed not to find in it what I had, so I resigned myself to keep looking only to come, some years later, back to the ringing logic of that song.

I saw the sense of what Gene was saying. I watched the weather come. I told myself that Jane hadn't had enough time to get to me in any other way than does an abstraction. She brought with her, as did Gene, the filthy lucre of the world I had rejected. Gene brought the surprise and focus of a genie. Jane brought an appreciation of the thoroughly incomprehensible that I later needed to accommodate Arvin. For each I needed to let go of where I was and follow them. I wasn't used to getting in step with anyone else. Now I think Jane had to die to certify her story. I could trust her dead. Alive, I had all the suspicions of a rat suddenly encountering fine cheese instead of the usual garbage. Sniff, sniff. And I was gone, poisoned or not. My metaphors fail me.

So Gene broached the subject that there might be a fist in the glove of my contacts.

"And just who are these people who have the manuscript now?" he asked.

I thought that explaining the whole Kraft family would not be a useful expenditure of energy at this time. How to set up a frame for Salome? How Arvin? So I explained that I had been contacted by the owners of the manuscript and then told to wait until they contacted me. I did know that they said they wanted at least a million dollars for it. And that they wanted to keep the deal secret and private and off any kind of official record—governmental or otherwise.

Gene nodded. "So if we came up with the manuscript and wanted to give it to the Newberry, we'd have to come up with a story for it too. That complicates things since we are not just a few, our consortium, and we'd all either have the same story or not all have all the information. Ruses, as you know, professor, are always more complicated than the truth."

We discussed which ruses might make the most likely story. There was: found in the trash, discovered in a curiosity shop, sold by a disappearing criminal, the South American connection (eyebrows raised for this one), and then variations on European flea markets (seller never came back again) and Russian contacts for a wealthy collector who needed to sell for quick cash (decide here on the amount of cash). All contingencies result in the consortium dealing on behalf of Melville scholars everywhere and, not incidentally, having themselves a significant, multi-year tax deduction.

Gene waved away the particular choices until later. "So do we have a deal? You'll call me when you need to exchange money for the manuscript? In the meantime, I'll take the deal to my group and see what I can come up with. You get a firm price and try to see the rest of the manuscript."

I said, sure, why not? The rain came in, but the land couldn't get any wetter than it was. The eaves dripped, the geraniums drank, the shore birds preened in freshwater, and I sat as the genie left in a cloud of smoke, back to his lantern, I supposed.

Smoke and dreamscape of undiscovered manuscripts: what do we think we are finding when we find out what a writer intended? I'm certain Jane and Gene and Godalming were not interested in what Melville thought first before he crossed it out and wrote in something else. Scholars care because with lots of emendations we think we get an idea of what all that revision was moving toward. The vision of the revision as the act of writing itself revealing to Melville what he was trying to mean—that's scholar's gold. But Godalming gave me the sense that he was contemplating owning some pearl of great price, an object, a talisman with which he could bewitch the world into admiring him. I still think of him as an evil troll, all gesture and posing and nefarious plot. On the other hand, Arvin, whom I thought physically resembled something Wagnerian in the troll family, had nothing troll-like about him even when he pulls the hood of his sweatshirt too tight around his face.

Rather than evil, he seems to become beatific, even approaching St. Francis deep in his monk's cowl. And so their inclinations seem to hang from them like destination tags. Strange fruit. And Jane just clouds my mind, and I get no clear literary view of her.

I always suspected the rat on the garbage heap. I mean that becoming a scholar for me was turning my back on the garbage heap in hopes I wouldn't have to engage the rat in any meaningful way. I mean . . . my sense of the activity of the world as a garbage heap offends even me. What superior claptrap I am capable of in my own defense! When I was in my thirties, I believed it most strongly—believed that I had chosen to be one of the chosen and then worked myself away from the world into the sweet aroma of libraries and the creak of chalk expended in the name of enlightenment, driving out the devils of ignorance and shallow thinking. What a perfect prig I'd found to pursue in the making of myself. Now I am only angry and don't know why.

Arvin comes riding in on the coastal bus and brings with him some antidote. I'm not sure why but I find myself laughing in his presence as if he had brought with him some silly sense at the base of the world, some religious foundation sorted out of the ether like a text revealed that certified God's goofiness. Arvin is not God's love but God's hilarity. He brings the cosmic message that we are all silly shits. Or that's what I needed him to bring, anyway. I think there's the scholar's way; and I think there's Arvin's way—the way of the meatball and what the meatball means.

I love competence better than I love my country, my ideals, myself. I think it is the one certifiable piece of evidence of the mind of God—a thing done well, built beautifully, handled and concocted. I think there are formal beauties in art that are discernible, and I think these carry over into human conduct and inform the way we act toward each other. We cannot only know competence but do it as well. The standard is always there. Enter Arvin to this competence.

Arvin slept off the long bus ride, the airplanes, the spaghetti.

He woke up looking puzzled and unsure. I watched him from the kitchen unfurl from the couch and begin the job of translating his surroundings like a horse let out of its trailer into a strange pasture. He still didn't see me. He checked the contents of his backpack, sniffed it, then closed it. Then he, and it seemed to me this was a disciplined move, checked out the next ring of his vision, the couch, the end table, my ragged chair, then moved out a ring to the broken TV, the bookcases, the detritus of my life. And once this was all included, ring by ring, he looked up and saw me in the kitchen, saw me watching him.

He pointed at me and then said, "There you are."

I nodded.

"I need to know what you plan to do about the papers my family has. Do you remember my sister, Salome?"

I said that indeed I did remember Salome as well as the rest of his family and the Triscuits with summer sausage. He seemed satisfied that I could bring up the details.

"But do you know about Salome?"

His eyebrows arched with the question as if to know about Salome might be a complicated and maybe impossible task without being a member of the Kraft family. I admitted as to not knowing any more about Salome than my day with the family had given me.

"Well, you need to think about Salome all the time that she's around. She told me that she requires this, she needs me to think what she would want me to be doing and then do that. For a long time I got up in the morning thinking about Salome and what she wanted me to do. Then Carl told about robots and showed me some pictures, and I knew that was what robots always did. They got their thinking done by whoever controlled them. When I told Carl that Salome wanted this or that, why then he'd bring up the robot stuff. The monkey stuff was bad enough, but I got on to that. The robot was harder, but once I found out about robots, I didn't want to be one anymore."

I got Arvin an orange soda, three ice cubes, the way he asked for it in the restaurant. I was in the presence of a kind of competence that I hadn't had much experience with before, but I recognized it just the same—the control of the disparate, the thematic connections, the accidents that were accommodated into the structure.

"Salome has part of the papers, but she thinks she has more than she really has."

Arvin now was speaking with an orange mustache and one finger raised like a cartoon lecturer.

"She has the beginning of the papers, then she has just old paper without any writing on it. Then she has a few pages at the end with not much writing on them. I have the rest. Salome thinks I tell her everything like a robot, but I don't. Salome thinks she's my mother. I used to think she was too. So I asked my other mother, and she cried. I didn't ask again because she never cries for anything else, even when Ben wrecked the car and scratched up his face with broken glass."

So I asked him if I could buy the papers from him or should I talk to Salome. He studied the question for a while, attended to the orange soda, swirled the ice cubes. Arvin said he would tell me about the papers more as soon as he had taken his time. Now he would like to see some fishing boats again if we could do that. So we did.

Arvin

When I first set eyes on the papers, after I broke a few pages because they were like powder and like glass, then I read some and then some more. I read about the man who had his teeth filed to points. I thought that might be a fine thing for me to do. Then I could show the teeth to Salome or Ben and make growling noises, and they'd leave me alone. I think they would look like shark teeth. I found a shark tooth once at the beach, but Ben and Carl took it and said it was too sharp for me to have. When I found a broken jack knife, I didn't show it to either of them.

The writing was easy to read after I studied it a long time. Every day I tried to read a few words, and then every day the reading got easier and easier until I could read lots of it. I kept it a secret because so many times I ran to one of them with what I found and like the shark's tooth they took it away. This time I kept the secret. And the longer I kept the secret the easier it was. I liked to walk past any one of them — after I learned not to smile because of when Carl gave me the Indian burn — and pretend I had something in my pocket that they couldn't see. A small magic something that was like the papers, that could get me out of trouble, could save my life again.

When I was small Carl had to take me along everywhere he went. I think that made him mean later. He waited until we were out of sight of the house, and then he'd tie a leash around my neck and make me heel. This made him mean because when we got home I told mother that I wasn't a dog. She said of course I wasn't. Who said I was? And I told on Carl, told that he made me heel and sit and stay, and I didn't mind because I could do all those things fine, and Carl gave me pats on the head and treats for doing them, but I didn't like being called a dog. Doing dog things was all right. Dogs pooped on our lawn and killed the bushes by peeing on them. I never did that even though Ben and Carl sometimes peed in the backyard.

I thought of the papers as a present to me. All the dead Krafts thought maybe I needed something to keep up with my brothers, and they gave me a present. After the pointy teeth part in the papers, I liked the ghost part at the beginning. I think it was about ghosts, anyway. I thought I was spying inside the walls, but I was like the words in the papers — something inside something else like olives with the red thing inside. I can't even say how much fun it was knowing about the papers. It was like when you look around at a birthday party and everyone has a party hat on, and they've had them on so long that no one is thinking about the party hats any more, just wearing them like nothing was special. That kind of fun. Even laughing isn't enough to hold how much fun it is.

So talking to Professor Rhinoceros about the papers and knowing he couldn't get them without me — that was fun in the same way. The hard part was leaving my family behind. Everything I knew was there in that place and in that house. On the bus ride from Portland and then down the coast I had the feeling that I was in a mirror since all the water and sun were reversed from where they should be. Carl spent a whole afternoon once explaining about mirrors to me. He was very interested in mirrors and how they worked and what they did. After a while everything he said seemed to come together, but I couldn't remember exactly how they worked. I started to like mirrors the same way he did, and I couldn't walk by one without thinking about what they did. He pretended to give me a test the next day about what he told me. I don't think I did very well on his test. He just walked away in the middle of it when I made up answers because I couldn't remember about refraction and reflection and things like that. But I got the idea of mirrors like I got the idea of the papers. I thought about it this way: the thing (whatever it was, mirrors, papers) wasn't in my head, and then it was. I had learned it to be there with the other things in my head.

My plan always was to go to Mexico. It was not only the

meatballs I read about there but also how I could live on a little money for a long time if I was careful. It was later when Salome was trying to talk me out of the papers and she said my plan was foolish because I didn't know how to speak Spanish and couldn't live there unless I could speak Spanish. I knew *albondigas*, so that would be a start. Like the mirrors, the rest would come the way it always had. I knew I needed thousands of dollars, the more of them the better.

The professor and I went out to see the fishing boats because I told him I wanted to see the boats from this coast, if they were the same as the ones I'd seen on the other side of the country. The boats were different and the names were different too. The Pacific boats were smaller. The Atlantic boats were uglier.

I said to the professor about the boats and he said, a bunch of words but I think he meant that he never looked very close at the Atlantic boats, and so he couldn't say one way or the other. I repeated what I said in case he hadn't heard me so that he'd know what I know. I was used to people not listening to what I said. My family usually began looking away — at a clock or something else — as soon as I tried to tell them something. None of them could slow down and listen to me, so I think they all thought I was dumber than I really was. But Professor Rhinoceros just laughed and said he was laughing at himself. Of course, he said, you, meaning me, would know that better than I would. He was different than my family but sadder. It seemed to me that there might be something missing in his life. Not like meatball sandwiches were in mine because I could get one if I needed it. More like a person is missing a finger or a hand. There was a boy in the third grade who was missing a hand and no one ever talked about it ever. I found that strange and one day I asked him what happened to his hand. He said there was an accident when he was a baby and his hand got crushed, but now he almost never thought about it. He couldn't remember when he had two hands. He did everything with one hand faster than I could with two, even batting a baseball. So the professor seemed like that to me. He was missing something, and whatever it was had been missing a long time.

But he did listen to me, maybe because he wanted the papers. The reason my sister would listen to me, or Ben too, was to get something from me. And with the wanting, the professor was sad. Carl was sometimes sad too, and he didn't want to talk to anybody when he was. I noticed after a while that right after he was sad he was mean. I learned to steer clear of him after the sadness. The professor just seemed to me to be missing something and then sad and then . . . not mean like Carl but not there really, absent like in school, but with a smile on his face. I was wondering about the missing part and made a note to ask him later. He asked again if the papers were safe, that sometimes they had sudden rainstorms on this coast, and storms could come up, and there weren't always good weather reports. I said it was okay and the papers were safe enough. Finally he shook his head and said okay, too. He said he wouldn't worry about it anymore since I was in charge of it.

There was a message on his phone thing when we got back. It was Salome saying to keep a lookout for me, that I had stolen money from her, that I was missing and capable of traveling clear across the country, that Professor Thorne was very often the topic of my conversation after his visit and Arvin, me, might want to talk to you (him) about something you never could tell. She talked fast like there wouldn't be enough room on the thing for what she had to say, and she had to hurry up and say everything. After we both listened to it, the professor looked at me for a long time and then asked me what I thought. Should we tell her where I was? I said that we should wait a while because she wanted the papers too but didn't know it yet. When he looked puzzled, I said that she thought she had most of the papers and hadn't found out yet that she didn't, and she'd be mad as hell when she did, so let's not tell her just yet. So I didn't call my family, he said, when I said I was going to? I didn't. He was right, and I couldn't say that anymore. I just wanted time to get used to being here, I said, and then I explained again how everything took me just a little bit longer, but if I had enough time then I could work almost anything out myself. And I didn't steal from Salome—the money to come across the country. I borrowed it. And he believed me, I think. Sometimes it seemed to me that the world was slow, and I was the fast one even though I knew better.

Ben almost never spent time deviling me. I think because Carl said I was his since we were closer in age. And then because Ben got very interested in the weather. Each time we sat down to the table Ben gave the weather in some other part of America. It was 53 degrees today in Billings, Montana, he'd say. Later it was places like Indonesia and Poland and then Arctic and Antarctic weather. I started to like his little weather reports, but I could see that it was driving Salome nuts. He said it was too bad that the big rains came so early, and then he would wait for us to ask. Where? I'd say. And he'd tell us where and how much. There was so much to say about the weather that he wouldn't run out of things to say. But one time he just sat there like a bump on a log. That's what he called me—a bump on a log because I didn't do enough for him, I guess. But this day he just sat there like a bump and even Salome waited for him to get it over with. He didn't say anything though. His weather reports had become like saying grace was for other families. I once ate at a cousin's house, and I expected someone to tell the weather somewhere before we ate, but they said grace. I listened all the way through about the God and Jesus parts thinking that maybe the weather would be at the end, but it wasn't. Ben just sat that one day while we waited. Then he took a deep breath and sighed and said there was not going to be weather today. Or ever, because the world was coming to an end, and weather didn't make any difference anymore. Then it looked like he was crying, but no noise came out. When he stopped, we all ate and pretended that nothing had happened. After dinner I took his hand and didn't say anything, and we walked around the block, the big block, not the short way down the alley and across—the long way. I didn't say anything because I didn't know what to say. He didn't say anything either, but after that when he was around he wouldn't let Carl devil me like before when he would just walk away, and Carl would start on me. I should have gone to Ben with the papers, and I would have if not for Salome's pen and what it made me do.

I think the professor didn't know about Ben and the weather reports, but he asked me about the weather on the Atlantic coast and told me about the Pacific coast weather, and it made me feel right at home. Ben had gone into the family construction business when his weather reports stopped. After that we'd just all start eating once Salome did. I missed Ben's reports.

The professor told me that he and some friends wanted to go together and buy the papers from me, but they needed all the papers, the part Salome had too. They wanted to give them to a big library so everyone could see them. He said the papers were worth a lot of money especially to some people. Maybe there were people who wouldn't be nice that would pay me even more than he could get. It was up to me to decide since I found the papers. He wanted to know how many of the papers Salome had, and I told him about that much and showed him a pinch with my fingers. All the rest I had. I told him again that whatever we were going to do about the papers I'd have to think over for a while since I didn't want to do anything very fast or before I could wrap my head around it all ways. He said I could take as much time as I wanted, but Salome didn't give us very much time, not the time I needed.

Thorne

Salome came into Newport like a winter storm: first, the leading edge sent us scattering for shelter and then the main part came on shore to howl and reduce us to nature's slaves, slam the old time fear into us, bring us low. She came with Ben and Carl and Mrs. Kraft stone silent around her like thunderheads.

Salome came—storm apart, once she was there I kept thinking of the severed head dripping blood—and filled my apartment while the rest of us scrambled for remaining space. She occupied the center and pinned Arvin against the chair. He sat. She explained to Arvin (and apparently, to me) that she had discovered that many of the pages were missing from the Melville manuscript, and that she was sure that I had not been unscrupulous toward her family and had not taken advantage of her brother's limitations in this matter. She was willing to take back all the papers and forget about the affair. Now. Her storm-cloud posse did what surrounding she didn't with her words. Arvin slumped lower into the chair, and at one point he looked as if he had somehow begun a chameleon's process of changing colors to disappear into his landscape.

Her voice was tactile and textured like burlap. She wrapped it around Arvin as he tried to mix molecules with the chair fabric.

"Arvin," she intoned. Carl and Ben guarded their luggage. Mrs. Kraft blinked. I found myself wondering if I could fit out the kitchen window should it come to that. "Arvin, will you get the papers now, please." It wasn't a question.

She was biblical and New England. She might have fixed herself softer and even courted alluring had she a mind for it. But she had, cross-country flight notwithstanding, achieved a sleek and efficient look like a working vehicle—a fire truck, a police cruiser. Her badges and emblems announced her official capacity: her auburn hair was pulled back and dominated in ways her mother hadn't managed, her beige cardigan appeared bulletproof, her skirt ran to the middle of her calf coming directly off significant hips. She had tied a green scarf around her neck, and the effect was more cowboy than accessory. She folded her hands beneath her breasts, and then, to see Arvin shrink, some kind of invisible rays fired out of her chest to command Arvin's compliance.

I tried to think when I had seen a comparable woman or read about one in literature. She beggared the human imagination in her looming. I searched Emile Zola, Henry James and Edith Wharton finally before giving up. Then I knew where I had seen this potency before. My first grade row partner Kitty Wells who looked words up in a dictionary faster than anyone else in class. She was undefeated. Her mother sent her each day to school in another fresh smocked dress where she performed miracles of speed reading and dictionary searching. I resigned myself to a perennial second place or worse. There was Kitty, and there was the rest of us. The summer after second grade she evaporated without a word, and I moved into the vacated throne as a quick study. But I always knew somewhere out there was Kitty, and I could merely occupy the throne until she returned.

That is, Salome in my apartment sent me time traveling for a template by which to judge what I was experiencing. I couldn't see Arvin's face, but his body had shrunk so significantly that I assumed his head must now be the size of an orange. From my vantage point halfway into the kitchen, Arvin's hooded sweatshirt might be a pile of crumpled rags on my shabby chair. Salome waited and then crossed and re-crossed her arms to give Arvin time to rise and follow her command.

From the chair came Arvin's voice soft but clear in a monotone as if he had rehearsed the line. "He doesn't have the papers, Salome. I do." The heap of rags stirred.

"I assumed you did, Arvin. Now get them for me please." The please hung in the air without civility again. It was a please without if-you-please in it.

We all watched the pile unfold out of the chair and stand up just short of Salome. Arvin reconstituted and plumped up. He said, "You can't have them. They're mine."

"They belong to the family, Arvin. You know that. Think of father now. Remember his picture on the mantel. Think of what he'd want you to do."

Arvin was drawing himself up taller, stretching from inside. Salome decided that the family needed to be alone at this moment and asked me if I would leave them alone—*en familia*—to work out this little problem. I thought two things simultaneously: one, I want to see this so I'm not leaving, and two, I would return to find Arvin devoured and his bones scattered along the baseboards so I'm not leaving. I backed into the kitchen to give the family room but said I'd stay. I thought Arvin deserved a little moral support even though he might be eviscerated. Salome shot me an ur-look, the one John the Baptist got, but she didn't pursue the unsavory prospect of throwing me out of my own apartment.

Arvin made his case the best he could. He would sell his part of the papers and go to Mexico. That was the long and short of it. He claimed to be ready to go including having a passport. Then he thought better of the claim and retrieved his passport from his backpack and waved it as substantive evidence of his plans. Salome pulled out the father card once again but to no visible success. She moved closer to Arvin and began what I recognized from my conversations with him as "the talk." Her voice assumed a new tenor and tempo with staccato punctuations in which his status as a human being was at stake, his duty to his family, his ounce of decency, his very soul. Ben and Carl cringed as if she had trapped them against a wall, too.

Arvin repeated his plans almost word for word as if he had found the proper combination and didn't need any restatement, no rhetoric and improved syntax. Here's what I'm going to do he said. You can't stop me. Here's what will happen.

Salome interrupted him and reached out to hold his shoulder, but he recoiled as if her hand had turned into a snake. "Arvin, your mother wants you to give the papers back." He looked her directly in the face. "*I* want you to give them back. I am your mother, Arvin, and I want them back. We didn't tell you before because there was no reason to confuse you. Ben and Carl suspected, but now they know too. I am your mother, and I insist that you give me the papers now, Arvin."

Arvin grew even taller somehow. He waited, and I could feel his cogitating. Then he said, "I knew that already. I could only be the way I was because you are the way you are. I know how that works. I know that song."

Carl and Ben looked at each other slowly like two parrots turning to gaze from their perch.

Arvin said, "It doesn't matter who is my mother. I thought about that already. I want the money to go to Mexico. You can't take the papers I have."

"Arvin!" Salome snapped. "Arvin, stop before you destroy us all." She looked at her mother, her first sign that she might be looking for help. "You don't understand, Arvin. It's not just money. We owe somebody some money, and if they aren't paid they'll harm our house and business. Maybe even us, Arvin. They'll hurt us. Any one of us they please. If we don't pay them . . ."

Salome looked at me. "Tell Arvin, Mr. Thorne. Tell him about people who hurt other people because they can't service a debt. Tell him about strong-arm tactics and bullying, Mr. Thorne. Arvin holds the key to the family's well-being. We are besieged on all sides, Professor. There are mean people who make money easy to borrow and then are relentless in their pursuit of repayment. The story is old. Tell him about Shylock and Dostoyevsky's pawnbroker, Professor." She pointed to Arvin, then opened her hand as if to give him the power.

Arvin had found an impregnable position and sat down again to rest his stretched legs. Salome turned her back to him. "They hold a lien on the papers. And whatever value the papers have, they own a fixed percent. If the papers are all together, they are

135

more valuable. If the papers . . ." She stopped and looked at her family one by one. "If the papers become more valuable somehow, then they stand to reap even greater rewards. Do you see our position, Professor? Or is this all too worldly for you?"

Salome's taunt came out of her fragile position, but she knew buttons like a mongoose knows how grab a cobra. Ah, my worldliness, my failure to know the world, and so instead I have engaged its writings. My secondhand world that could tell you which text has taken on which moral principle but not how that principle decocts in the great brewing of life itself. I had long ago decided that there had been a surfeit of humans actually living out the miseries and joys of life and that somebody needed to stand back and observe. I would take my dramas on a manageable scale—divorce, Jane's death and its inherent distance from me. I would keep the counsel of barrooms and leave the adventures for others. Ask me about the inks or the paper, Salome. Ask me how the English typesetters refused to understand or set some American words and changed the text as they set it. Salome, I could recite chapter and verse to you from inchoate copyright laws of England and America. Salome? Salome? Are you listening? Of course you aren't. You are frozen in the middle of the room now with your hands on your hips watching Arvin petrified but wide-eyed with his new powers, his brothers reconsidering all Arvin's established limitations. She ups the ante. "Arvin, they'll kill us one by one if we don't . . ." She checks her audience. "If we don't do as they say." Power shift. Not your father or mother or your putative mother or your brothers, but it is "they" who demand this from you, Arvin, not me. Salome regroups with one hand on her mother's shoulder, the other touching the uncomfortable Carl's arm. She links up.

I stood transfixed, enthralled by the Krafts like a text can enthrall. What hadn't mattered to me—who got the manuscript, who got money, who got credit—now had a glowing urgency, and I couldn't get enough of it. It was exciting to have the Kraft family playing out ancient dramas in my humble living room. All I had cared about is how fast the manuscript became public—a copy would do. Then suddenly, though I was still aware that I might be able to fit out the kitchen window and leave the whole encounter behind, I didn't want to. I was willing to stay through wholesale destruction and mayhem. Thinking I might just prefer it.

Salome had played father card, mother card, ancestral family card. Now she was flipping through the deck to see what else was there. She came up with her Mont Blanc pen.

"Do you know, Arvin, how much that pen of mine cost? The one you destroyed by playing with it? That one. The one I asked you repeatedly to avoid out of respect for other people's property?" She caught him looking up from the chair, saw his return look, knew she had struck gold. "Tell me how hard you had to push on it to break it the way you did. Tell me did you think, 'now I'll break Salome's pen on purpose'? Did you think that if you smashed my pen then you'd really hurt me, pay me back for taking care of you, helping you get along in the world? Do you remember in first grade when those children were mean to you the first day and I went to talk to the teacher and the students' parents? It was raining and sleeting, and I went because I couldn't stand seeing you hurt."

Arvin remembered and squirmed. He had lost the length he'd stretched up to at the beginning of the encounter. "I didn't try to break it. I just wanted to . . ."

Salome waited. "Just what? Just wanted to hurt me? So you pushed harder, then harder, didn't you? It must have taken a very strong hand to break that gold nib. Or did you slam it with something? A hammer or pliers? Is that what you did, Arvin? Did you break it apart just to watch the ink run all over the linen tablecloth? Was that it? Was it an experiment to see how much you could hurt me?"

Arvin looked skewered. "I didn't mean to break it . . . I just . . ."

"That pen can't be replaced, Arvin." Now the repeating of his name became like a twisting of the steel. "Arvin, you need to think about what you owe me. What you owe all of us—mother, Ben,

Carl. Me. We have taken care of you and protected you, Arvin, all your life, and each one of us has something that we have forgiven you. We let it slide because we love you, Arvin. Now you owe us your love in return. Get us the papers, Arvin."

Mrs. Kraft shifted her feet as if she were going to go toward Arvin. But Salome reached out to push back the hood on his sweatshirt, maybe to caress him. Arvin rose up out of the chair propelled by some preternatural power of his own making and flew past me and out the kitchen window. I ran to the window to see how he had fared in the drop to the ground, but he was on the ground and scampering across the yard over a wooden fence and out of sight.

I looked and the family still stood where they had been the moment Arvin took flight. It was as if they had been frozen, as if he had used up all their ability to move by his own sudden draining of all kinetic juice from the room. Then Salome slumped into the still warm chair. Ben and Carl melted onto the couch. Mrs. Kraft looked vacantly out the window. I thought of asking them if anyone was hungry but didn't. Would you like something to drink? Can I console your bitter hearts in any way?

Arvin

Salome had grown like a giant in that room, and I couldn't breathe. I couldn't find just one thing to think about while she was that big. She took away all my thinking place, and I was lost in all the thinking every thing at once with no space between anything. I went out the kitchen window without thinking if it was open or what was outside. I must have noticed it was open before because I went right past the professor and out his window and down the side of his building holding on to a rain gutter. I didn't begin thinking again until I was down the hill and through some blackberry bushes and across a bunch of streets.

Salome was my mother she said. Since that was surprising and I didn't know what to think about it, I just let it go past like I always knew it. I know better than to just jump at something like that the way I used to and then find that I was a fool. Once Carl made me a sign with his special writing with its fancy curls and things so you couldn't really read it very well, old-fashioned writing like on castles. It said Foole, but I couldn't read it so I taped it on my door thinking it was a fine present he'd made me. Salome took it down and told me it said something bad and just forget about it. Carl told me later what it said, and he thought it was a good joke but it wasn't. Carl had to listen a long time to Salome for that, and he hated listening more than all of us put together. He told me what the sign said and then didn't talk to me for more than a week. He said he was trying to tell the truth like Salome always told him to do. Carl said that now that he knew no one meant what they said, he'd just do as he pleased. And, I guess he did.

I went toward the ocean after I went out the window and thought about Salome as my mother. Then what would mother be? Could a person have two mothers? Was Salome the mother of Ben and Carl too? Who was my father? Ben had explained to me about having babies, what the father did, what the mother did. Was my father in the picture over the mantel my father with Salome? Was my mother my grandmother? That's what I thought about when I could get my brains back together. I never knew anyone who could grow big and fill up a room like Salome could. If she was my mother then could I learn how to do the growing too?

The sand was wet and cold. I walked up a long beach with the wind at my back. I knew about walking against the wind on a beach so that it would be at your back when you went back home. But I didn't care and walked with the wind at my back right away because it felt good to be pushed down the beach, like coasting on a bicycle. You know you have to pedal again, but you just like coasting without pedaling for as long as you can. I knew Salome would send Ben and Carl after me rather than chase me herself. She always sent them after me since when she found out I could run away from her even in the backyard, and if I didn't want her to catch me, she couldn't. Her skirts always made her seem slow and big. I felt like a hummingbird sometimes, faster than anything around.

I walked away from the bridge too. Sometimes when I thought about a secret so hard, I'd give it away by looking at the hiding place or starting to say what I shouldn't. That happened to me so many times that Carl and Ben took away all my secrets all the time. Sometimes they'd just check to make sure I wasn't hiding something they wanted to know about. When I found the papers I learned to think of something else, repeat it over and over to myself, so if I got surprised by them then that something else would come out. Blurt. Carl said to me, "Blurt, Arvin. Give it up. Just blurt." I learned to blurt only what I had been repeating to myself. Jennifer Tillman peeing in the backyard I considered a kind of gift from God. I don't know how I thought of it to tell Carl to get away from the Indian burn.

The longer I walked with the bridge at my back the better I felt. There were some other people on the beach, and I could walk as fast as I wanted near the water where the sand was hard. Walking in the soft sand reminded me of dreams where everything is slow like water standing on a tabletop. Just standing, not going anywhere. And then I thought that Ben and Carl might look for me on the beach doing exactly what it was I was doing. Of course they would, and they would come after me. They know I like the ocean and the sand. I made my way up to the grassy places away from the water. I still didn't know where I was going.

Once I ran away from home without knowing where I was going. There was no reason to do it, no special reason except that I had heard the idea, run away from home. I didn't even know why people would run away from home, but I guessed they really did because I heard about it. So I decided to run away from home— from the house I loved and those people who fed me and washed my clothes even if Carl was mean to me sometimes. Everybody has somebody mean to them sometimes is what I figured.

One of Ben's favorite things to do to both me and Carl was to read to us from an old book he had of fairy tales. But these weren't the happy fairy tales, he always said. These were the real fairy tales from long ago, and sometimes things didn't turn out so good for bad children. He liked to read about the German children who were bad, and when they fell asleep someone, I forget who it was, came and cut their thumbs off. There was a picture of all the children asleep with their heads lined up on big pillows and a guy holding up a knife. After Ben read the story, I sat looking at my hands for a long time and tried to imagine them without thumbs. Carl taped his thumbs to his hands for a while to see what it would be like. I wouldn't let him tape mine down that way. Now I can't remember what the children did that was so bad. Maybe it was an uncle who cut their thumbs off. We didn't have any uncles, I think, but one aunt.

What was Salome going to do, anyway? It is illegal to put people, even your brother, in the garbage disposer.

There were small birds in the sand, and no one could see us.

I walked until the fog started to come off the water. I found my brains while walking, but I wasn't ready for Salome again. Was she just saying she was my mother to get me to obey her? Why didn't Ben or Carl ever say anything about her, that she was my mother? Ben would do a German accent when he read the thumbs story: "Vee, vill cut your sums off," he'd shout and then jump up. But he never said anything about Salome being my mother.

When Professor Thorne came to our house and sat at the table with us, I don't know why, but I felt I was on his side against my family, and I didn't even know what side was his side. I didn't know then about the people on the phone who made Salome all crazy so no one could even talk to her. I knew that for the first time someone outside our family seemed right and my family wrong. Once that started, everything was different, maybe like Carl and the truth.

On the sand walking away from the bridge, I expected Carl and Ben at any moment, but I was ready for them. They couldn't make me do anything I didn't want to. My whole life I had to do what they said even if I didn't want to do it. Mother, my first mother, always said to obey Ben and Carl and I wouldn't get lost or hurt myself, so that's what I did. It took a long time for me to know that obeying wasn't the best thing for me. Professor Thorne sat at the table looking at his small food, and I felt exactly like he felt looking out over my family's faces. Salome, my mother. That explains a lot. Her lips straight across her face like Carl used to draw the lips on dragons; they didn't go up or down. Carl said dragons didn't smile or frown because they weren't human beings. Salome's lips were dragon lips.

The beach sand blew, and I got on my knees to watch it. The top grains skipped over the other ones. The smallest ones flew by, off to go somewhere else. I wanted to go somewhere else too, but I needed the money from the papers I found. Mexico would be the best place because I didn't think anyone could tell me what to do there because I didn't speak the same language they did. I tried to imagine no one telling me what to do, no one making me do things. Would I know what to do without anyone telling me? I felt some sand in the palm of my hand. Could I find the very best grain and separate it from the other ones? I rolled them around until I saw a perfectly clear one bigger than the other ones. I thought it must be a diamond, just tiny. I pushed away the other grains and left just the one in the middle of my palm. Then I put it carefully in my pocket and tried again. This time I found a yellow grain, small and flat, and said that it would be the best of all. I put it in my pocket with the other one. I remember being on a beach with Salome, and I found a stick and then another stick and then another one. Pretty soon I had a whole collection of sticks that went together and gave them to her as a present. She said thank you Arvin and pretended to put them in her skirt pocket but really dropped them on the beach behind her back. I said those were the best sticks of the beach, and she said she knew. I said really, those are the best ones and they go together. She said she knew that too. I asked her why she threw them away then, and she said she didn't really throw them away, just left them on the beach for someone else to find again. And that was that.

I used to sing a sorting song to myself when I sorted my laundry by color or white. Salome made us boys keep our laundry separate in two hampers and I was always putting the wrong one in the wrong hamper, I guess (or Carl or Ben were doing it, but I was getting blamed). So to keep from losing track I sang a sorting song saying the name of the sock—colored or white—before I put it in the right place. It wasn't a complicated song; it was just, "white one goes here, colored one goes there," but when I was singing it was easy to keep track of what I was doing. And as long as I sang I sorted perfectly, so I knew it wasn't me if the laundry from the boys was ever mixed. There on the beach with the wind blowing and my brothers coming I sang a song like the sorting song but just a song that helped with what I knew was coming. "Here comes Ben and here comes Carl," I sang. "They're coming to take me back with the wind in my face," I sang. I sang while I waited for them.

But instead, in about half an hour, it was Salome coming down the beach with her skirt blowing, and my other mother and brothers weren't with her. Her skirt came before she did in the wind, and she kept it down in front with one hand and the other held her hair. She floated toward me with her brown shoes, big and brown against the sand she kicked up. She doesn't see me yet, but I see her. I stopped the song I was using to get ready for Carl and Ben. I didn't have a song for Salome. I never have.

Thorne

Salome sat frozen for about twenty seconds then got up suddenly and brushing her brothers and mother aside, swirled out the door and down the stairs. Ben and Carl followed slowly while Mrs. Kraft took the chair her daughter had lately occupied.

"You know, Professor Thorne, Salome is not used to being denied under any circumstances. We talked about this in Seattle, though I didn't use her name. I said that it would be important to do this the way the family needed to do it. By the family I meant Salome. Since she was about fourteen years old she has been . . . headstrong is the old-fashioned word. I think the new way of talking about this is control freak, though I don't relish the freak part when speaking of my own daughter."

I asked her if Salome was really Arvin's mother or was that just her way of making him obey.

"Oh no, she *is* his mother, of course. Part of her headstrongness was apparent very early as a teenager, and Salome was curious about lots of things, sex being one of them. And then she wouldn't hear of an abortion. She wanted to hold the baby and look at it, she said. It seems right after that though that she lost interest and assigned the baby to me. It was her father who wanted to name Salome that name from the Bible, that wicked, wicked woman's name. He said it was a powerful name and a girl would thank us for the powerful name one day. Well, he never lived to see her assume her powerful name. That's the way life always goes. And by the time she was eighteen she was running our failing business and making it profitable again. Then Arvin was completely my responsibility except when Salome wanted to train him to be something or do something. Then she took an interest again."

I asked Mrs. Kraft about what she knew about the manuscript now.

"I know, Professor Thorne, only what Salome has told me. We

have, every one of us, except Arvin now apparently, given ourselves over to Salome's . . . what? Her power, her keen intuition. Maybe her freakish control. I don't know anymore. Sometimes I get so tired of the whole thing. It's as if I don't care at all how this turns out. But of course, I should care. These are my children, my blood. But I tire so easily these days. I just want to get this over with. Can you understand that, Professor? I know the manuscript is worth a great deal of money and that it belongs to my family. But there are . . . complications. Yes, complications like there are everywhere in life, you know. Salome can tell you about these if she wants to. But the long and the short of it all is that Salome will get the rest of the manuscript from Arvin—we have the remaining part. And then . . . and then what? I don't know and more and more I find myself not even curious as to how this will resolve itself. Do you ever just get very, very tired, Professor?"

I told her I did.

"No, I mean so tired it feels like your brain is worn out like an old pair of sneakers, the tongue lolling out, the shoestrings broken and tied so many times . . ."

Mrs. Kraft apparently got tired again just thinking about the old sneakers/brain and simply fell silent with a sigh right out of a German absurdist play—*Weltschmertz*. I put my hand on her shoulder, but she just stared straight ahead. I wanted to tell her about tired, the nature of tired, maybe how it had been theorized in literature—*Weltschmerz* and *ennui*—the great tediums of Russian literature. Then I wanted to tell her about Jane and the way Jane parsed the world, then came into my world with her parsing mechanisms—the engaging and beautiful, the past and morose—gaining and losing and how she measured all this *Moby-Dick* business against terra-cotta warriors and pre-Columbian jade masks. Anybody can be tired out, I wanted to tell her. How the Victorians figured boredom as a lack of inner resources, how Brett Hart's cowboy, Hemingway's hired killer, Stephen Crane's soldier all sighed her sigh. Outrage was one way out. Terror worked. And then somehow St. Anthony being fed by the animals in the woods occurred to me, and I thought I should tell her about that. I wanted her to feel better and perk up. Why? My own life was scrambled eggs. I could imagine Arvin scooting down the beach with the family in pursuit. Maybe they'd tree him eventually and then starve him down or, better yet, entice him down with meatball sandwiches.

Mrs. Kraft had gone comatose, overcome perhaps by her sadness. I was hoping that the encounter with the Kraft family might provide me more Jane revelations, but they wouldn't come. Jane had begun to seem a character in a book now, part of a larger literary pattern that surfaced and then disappeared and then surfaced in my life. It occurred to me—it seemed to be where I found myself now, a man to whom things occurred—that the ill wind surrounding the manuscript was unrelenting, on shore and building.

Mrs. Kraft vaguely comatose in my ragged chair, I supplied her with a glass of water and went out. I scanned the streets for signs of the Kraft clan—hunters and hunted—but came up empty. I thought I might call in Gene Anczyski. Call in Albert of the police force. Call in everybody I could think of. I kept thinking we all needed some subtler touch here, some mental kung fu to counter Salome, a ju-jitsu John the Baptist. I thought maybe biblical, encyclical: the New Testament, Pope John the XXIII and the prophecy of John the Divine.

I was thinking there was some part of the financial enterprise of the Kraft family that Salome was withholding. And I was sure it was hidden in the gloss on their finances she called DaGamma. This was a lender or a buyer of debts, or it was some kind of uber-insurance company dealing in high-risk loans that had come to be a partner to the Kraft family holdings. The questions that kept looming to me, looming like in the *Moby-Dick* chapter called, "Loomings," was whether DaGamma also dealt in subtle and surreptitious accidents or murders. Did this partner, this banking facility, also leave bodies in portable outhouses and nudge cars off the road on dangerous turns? Did they contract out thugs to scare the shit out of university professors, and/or add one professor to the list of carcasses piling up around the manuscript? And, how many bodies would constitute the curse of Ahab that would make the manuscript worth so much more than it actually was?

I had some experience with curses. There was an old woman in my hometown when I was growing up who lived in a depression in the land, in a basement. There was no top to her house, just the basement surrounded by a hole that had never been filled in after the initial excavation. Apparently she ran out of money after the basement was built, so she had the flat top covered in tarpaper and lived underground, maybe waiting for enough money from her children to continue construction. But as long as I was a child she lived like a fairytale witch down in the hole emerging only in the evening to scurry around the dirt pile that made up her yard. Weeds grew tall and vigorous in a kind of garden that mocked the surrounding houses with their manicured lawns and flowerbeds. For children she was the haunted house, the old witch, the ogre, the troll, the changeling that populated the evening parts of our brains and the stories that fetched out the evening light where nothing was entirely clear and anything was possible.

The curse. She cursed a boy, the boy who would stand in front of her house and throw gravel onto her driveway just be annoying. He was collecting dirt clods from the piles outside her house and lobbing them onto her flat, tarpaper roof where they burst with a satisfying *thunk* that seemed to use the whole basement structure as a bass drum. Over and over he lobbed one clod at a time and then moved on to having two clods in the air at once that descended on the old woman's drum with a one-two beat. Something in the starburst of dirt and the bass drum took over the boy's wits, and when he saw that he had collected an audience of fascinated kids across the street—me included—he began to play the old lady's roof like an inspired percussionist. Then she emerged from the hatchway right between clod bursts and pointed at him.

She began in low sounds with "scat" and "go away" and recognizable shooings that seemed to have no effect on the drummer. Then she switched to another language, a collection of gutturals and yelps and fricatives that repelled the raining clods at first. The boy missed with several clods. Then she pointed with both hands at the boy repeating the pointings as if she were throwing something at him straight from her shoulders. Over and over she jabbered and pointed and moved slowly toward the boy until she was perched on the edge of her flat roof. Her toes seemed to curl over the edge, and the effect of her advance was to scatter the audience on the other side of the street while it froze the boy with a clod in each hand. She kept up the stream of sounds until it carried in a steady rhythm that might have been a repetition, but the sound rained down on the boy until he finally broke and ran still holding a clod in each hand.

And so, I realized later, that was the first curse I had ever witnessed.

The boy became . . . different, other, then. Instead of the perennial pest and troublemaker, he became, first, diffident and seemed to melt into the background. Second, he seemed to lose speech, talking less and less, so that he not only avoided the other children but when encountered he seemed to have lost himself. He muttered. He finally fell silent, and summer nights when the other children ran jabbering and sweating through the neighborhood before bedtime, he was seen in the shadows and deep in the bushes peering out. At the time I thought he had simply continued on his road to strangeness. Later, a number of us who were witnesses the day of the curse decided that a curse from Mrs. Dahlman had altered the boy. He died at the age of thirty-four sitting at the breakfast table with his mother. He died of a massive heart attack and fell face first into a bowl of Cherrios. He had never married. He combed his hair like Elvis and worked at a body shop in town. Mrs. Dahlman was long dead when the curse worked its final evil on his clod-throwing life.

So I thought I knew about curses. Everyone saw it happen, the inexorable turn of the screw that drew that boy into the earth through his Cherrios.

The curse of Ahab was adding considerably to the value of the manuscript it turned out. Gene Anczyski rattled the wallets of his friends and out came a significant sum toward buying the manuscript as a deductible gift to the Newberry Library. But Salome, apparently with the help of some phone calls to DaGamma, came up with a new amount that the manuscript would cost now that the newspapers had picked up the curse. Now it was a notorious, even malevolent, stack of papers, but the fact remained that Salome didn't have it all; she had a little piece and Arvin had the rest.

Arvin

Salome didn't catch me. She didn't have to because she knew that Ben and Carl would find me eventually and fetch me back to her to answer. I watched her float down the beach with her skirt like a bubble trying to burst. She floated right by where I hid in the grass and sand. Because of the sand which is there, I kept thinking. You can't starve at the beach because of the . . .

Salome used to take us to the beach in Massachusetts, near a lighthouse that looked a little like the one in Newport. She said she was the general and we were her soldiers. Ben and Carl wanted to be captains and colonels, but I liked being a soldier. We marched down to the beach carrying the picnic baskets. Carl called them ammunition boxes. Ben didn't like marching behind Salome and tried running ahead, but she stopped him by throwing the blanket over him and wrapping him up in it. It was like a spider web I watched once inside the walls. A bug got caught, and then the spider came out of the wood where she lived and right down to wrap him up and leave him hanging in the web in a neat little package. Sand always smelled like clean dirt to me, dirt that had been scrubbed or something. Special white dirt.

Salome took an interest in me because I could sing. Singing seemed easy, I remember, and singing I could remember what I couldn't without singing. I think I was about eight or nine. My teacher sent a note home with me that my mother should listen to me sing my lesson. I sang it for both my mothers, then I sang it for Ben, too. They all clapped. But Salome clapped harder and smiled as if I had done a very special trick, and everything would be changed now. But that's all there was to it. I could sing things like addition problems and state capitols, and I would remember them. This was not enough for Salome, though. She wanted me to sing big math problems and then long lists of words. I could sing them but I couldn't remember them after because they were too long or too big or something. Then she looked at me in that way she had that made me feel like a farm animal, a pig, a goat, a goose. Then she walked away.

After trying to get her to pay attention to me for a long time, I suddenly found myself at age fourteen trying to get her to ignore me like she did most of the time Ben and Carl unless they had done something to make her mad. And she did, and that was when she became the boss of the business and spent all her time on that. They thought I didn't know who my mother was. I tried to be surprised at Thorne's house when she said she was my mother, and I should listen to her. But think I knew it some way before that.

I don't remember how old I was when I bought that bad toy. I don't even like to think about it, so I call it the bad toy. It cost too much and it was cheap. That's what Carl said after he saw it. If you looked inside with a flashlight you could see it was made from beer cans, Budweiser beer cans. The gears were beer cans, everything was beer cans, only it was painted on the outside to look like a spaceship or something. Except it had big wheels and sparks flew out of the back end. Carl said it looked like its butt was on fire and that's what made it run around in circles like that. I had to get every cent out of my bank to get that bad toy. After I got it, I sat in the backyard with it in my lap, and Salome saw me from the window and came out. She wanted to know where I got the bad toy, and I told her I bought it with my own money. She put her hand on my head and sighed. I felt like crying. I think she was going to ask me how much I spent for it but she stopped. I was twelve or thirteen, I think. Finally I noticed that if I sat with the bad toy on my lap and looked at it, I felt like crap — a fool, stupid. But if I didn't look at it I felt a little better. Then if I got it off my lap and behind me I felt even better. Then I got up and got a shovel and buried it about a foot deep at the end of the garden behind the garage where I wouldn't even be able to see the pile of dirt unless I went to the back of the garage looking for it. I felt much better. The bad toy was gone, I had no money, but I didn't feel like any kind of fool anymore. Things were undone. My foolishness was kind of gone. I'd find a way to get more money, and then it would be all undone. That was what I learned from the bad toy. I decided maybe it was worth the money.

When I decided to keep the money from the papers for myself, that and go to Mexico to get away from my family, I knew that I would probably make some "bad toy" mistakes in something as tricky as all this. But I knew too that I could fix most things if I had time to think. On the beach after Salome sailed by on the wind, I knew I didn't have the whole business very clear in my head. I had: Mexico, lots of money to live there, and sell the papers to get the money. I even had: hide the papers in the bridge. That one came at the last minute when I looked around in Newport and saw the bridge like a giant monkey bars up there, green and rusty and curved. I knew that I had to hide the papers somewhere before I sat down with Mr. Thorne or he might take them the way Carl and Ben took.

So I went back up away from the beach, across the highway, behind a restaurant and then down a hill near a lighthouse and a Coast Guard station. They wouldn't find me right away there, I was thinking. I need to find a way the keep Salome from just taking whatever she wanted from me. I need a place to think about things. I need to feel good about this like when that toy went in the hole and I covered it up a little at a time feeling better each second.

Thorne

They all came back without Arvin. He had just disappeared. Mrs. Kraft was not less comatose than when they left. Carl was agitated and pacing and muttering under his breath. Apparently he had covered the greatest distance looking for Arvin and now felt the most sinned against. Ben fell silent, on some wavelength close to his mother's flat line. He sat in a straight chair with his arms crossed while his brother paced and Salome publicly fumed.

"I'm holding you responsible, Professor Thorne." She had sand in her shoes and took one off and poured sand in my wastebasket. "Arvin is very impressionable, and I don't know what you talked about before we got here, but when he's not his gentle self, it's usually that someone put him up to something." She glared at Carl as if he would know what *that* was about. I protested briefly, but she sawed the air to stop me. "I know what you think you've been doing, but that's not what's happening. My mother told me about the Seattle performance for the police. And I can tell you now, more than ever, that you cannot involve them in this. You must not involve them. Do you understand? Do you? I don't think you do, so I'll tell you more than you need to know just to get you to stretch a little out of your secure little ivory tower."

Fuck you, Salome, you and your snit and your "I got woes you don't understand" load of crap, I wanted to say in a most unprofessor-like way. Fuck your posturing and sawing the air and cowing your brothers and your comatose mother while I'm at it. I hope Arvin scams you out of everything and leaves you hung out to dry on whatever clothesline you've got yourselves hanging from. Fuck that you're alive. Fuck your family back ten generations. I began to recall the curse of Ernulfus from *Tristram Shandy* and felt as if my fuck-yous were pretty lowbrow in literary comparison. I revised while she raged, revised toward Ernulfus: "May the Father who created man, curse her—May the Son who suffered for us, curse her—May the Holy Ghost who was given to us in baptism, curse her—May the Holy Cross which Christ for our salvation triumphing over his enemies, ascended—curse her. May the holy eternal *Virgin Mary*, mother of God, curse her—May St. Michael the advocate of the holy souls, curse her—May all the angels and archangels, principalities and powers and all the heavenly armies, curse her...May she be cursed inwardly and outwardly—May she be cursed in the hair of her head—May she be cursed in her brains, and in her vertex, in her temples, in her forehead, in her ears, in her eyebrows, in her cheeks, in her jaw bones . . . May she be cursed in all the joints and articulations of her members, from the top of her head to the sole of her foot, may there be no soundness in her . . ."

Salome slammed the door and left, left her family each in his or her own bilious, phlegmatic or rheumatic funk.

Slowly they reanimated and left my apartment together. I wanted to say to their backs: "Bye-bye. See ya." But I didn't, even as I pressed myself into action to call Gene and . . . and . . . together for this . . . what? Event, ceremony. I wanted company. The Kraft family one-on-one with a professor of suspicious social skills—well, that appealed only to my sense of apocalypse. I was thinking that Arvin had all the power until I saw Salome as his mother and Arvin vaulting out the window. Then I knew I was in over my head just in the presence of this family.

A cautionary tale that had happened to me not long ago:

It was the second beer that brought the bozos in. Standing next to each other they spoke as if they needed to be heard across the room and over the jukebox. They also had, I thought, that head shape that seemed to go with being assholes. Maybe there was something to phrenology. The loud, aggressive blowhards always had heads shaped something like a potato. Some might take exception to the possible Irish slur implied in this theory, but the fact remained, potato-headed people of any race, creed or persuasion always opened their potato-headed mouths, and out came something to shame civilization itself.

There were four of them. They didn't dress like coast denizens, more like tourists, escapees from high in the end zone at a college football game. The most potato-headed one was ordering his third beer and watching the bluster and noise as the men circled to look for a place in the bar to possess. I had seen this happen before and began to think what other bar might have a preferred seat left at this late, three-beer stage. Bup's Tavern was under construction and had no real preferred seating left at all. Jones Harbor would be packed with boatmen moaning over the price of crab at the dock. Sprouter, Blue Bill's Place, the Sip-'n-Sea, the Quarterdeck would be okay but bar stools only. The back booths at Liberty's Ketch were cold and you could grow old getting another beer. I thought I'd wait it out here.

The bozos got louder and louder, and I wondered what the beer supply at home would be like. Somewhere there was a library that served beer where a man could fall asleep with his head on a stack of fresh texts.

Suddenly one large oaf, less potato-headed than the others, who had gone long for a nerf-football pass from the smaller goof, crashed into my table spilling his beer into my lap.

"Jesus Christ," I said. I hadn't seen the large oaf coming.

"Hey man. Don't talk like that about my personal savior." It was the shorter guy, who had followed his pass and was challenging me across the sitting bulk of his wide receiver.

I sighed, got to my feet and the guy was yelling directly into my chest belligerently. "I said you. Yes, you. You talk like that around me and you've got to deal with me. The beer was an accident. No call to blaspheme in front of me. It's about respect. Yes, you." All said in one stream while poking me in the chest. Apparently this move had worked to get fights for the guy before because he returned to the beginning when he ran his words full circle and started over again this time poking insistently harder and harder with his short index finger.

I was backed up against the wall dripping my own beer with the finger-poking coming on stronger and stronger, but somehow the scene seemed projected in front of me, unreal as yet. I couldn't find my feet properly, and the poker had switched to knuckle thumping while I tried to gather myself and search for reality. *Whump. Whump.* The knuckle became insistent and the speech out of the potato-face had gone into the third go-round. I brushed at the knuckle thumping into my chest in exactly the same spot, and the thumping stopped. The guy had been waiting for a reply and had his first punch firmly in mind. And his second. He sucker-punched me from down low, catching me squarely under the chin and sending my head into the wall, a glancing blow. The second punch, thrown from above as I slipped down the wall, caught me in the forehead knocking my glasses across the room. I tried to find my glasses by feeling around in the beer, but the gold frames camouflaged themselves in the amber beer. I tried to stand up. From one wet knee I was lifting myself toward the light when the guy got in one last shot and caught me square in the side of the head. I went down.

The guy was thinking to do some kicking now that I was puddled in the spilled beer and out cold. His friends, led by the tight end who started it all, grabbed him and pulled him off after only one rib kick. I never even moved, crumpled like a heap of rags. The men left the bar quickly, hauling their buddy who still ranted about what he'd do to anybody he didn't like, who insulted his savior, his dog, his birth month, his. . . . The regulars helped me into a booth, but I still didn't come all the way conscious. They sat me up like a rag doll, and I drooled onto the seat. Finally they propped me in the corner of the booth and checked my eyes. They got whites. They ordered more beer to oil the decision about what to do next. One school said I just needed time to come around. A second, smaller, soberer group thought they should take me to the hospital though who should drive was another discussion. No one figured on going anywhere until hours from now when the night wound down toward closing.

While the discussion dragged on, I moaned and came around. I was rewarded with a fresh draft on the house but sat holding the cold glass to my head, beer dribbling down my face and on to my coat. The cold kept the throbbing to a diesel-engine level. I collected myself inside the pain and finally asked, "What the hell was that all about?"

"I never seen that crowd in here before. Shit, that little guy sure had a firecracker up his ass. I do think he might have done you some real harm, Professor, if his buddies hadn't a pulled him off. I don't know what got up his nose. What'd you say to get him that mad?"

I wiped at my temple where the skin had brightened to crimson. I shook my head. "I don't remember saying anything that would set him off like that. He kind of just came after me yelling about his personal savior or something. Then he hit me."

"*Commenced* to hit you," corrected one of the regulars. "Seems like he must of hit you a bunch before anybody could get over here. His buddies sure were quicker than the rest of us. Like they knew he would go off or something. He got his licks in and then began to try to kick the slats out of you. That's when they hauled him away just like a guy would put his dog on a leash to haul him away from a dog fight."

Without moving my head, I looked up at the guy giving this version of the fight. "I would guess that would stretch the meaning of dog fight or even fight. I don't remember participating in any fight. I *was* there for a beating though."

The regulars agreed that I probably had that right. Then they began to speculate about where those guys came from. There were two possible directions for the highest percentage of probability — north or south. If they had come from the east, they would have had to drive down from one of the old lumber towns now petered out in the Coastal Range. And those towns were so small almost everyone was known on the coast. There was a slight chance that these were a bunch of goons no one had run across before; an even slighter chance they were from the Willamette Valley on the east side of the range. After a moment thinking through the beer, through the logic, through my predicament, the regulars decided that this particular collection of scofflaws had most probably come from California.

"Well, yup. California would explain it."

"The big burns down there last summer drove some of 'em up here from what I can tell."

"Kind of like driving skunks out from under a shed with smoke. Then we'd try to herd 'em toward where we had a line of cat food—kibbles, you know—that we'd let set over night in antifreeze. They always went for it too. Made short work of polecats."

"Mothballs. My old man swore by mothballs to get skunks to move on. He'd just chuck a handful under the shed or smoke house–that was where they liked to hide—then those suckers would move out."

"I heard mothballs work on gophers and moles, too . . ."

"Oh, wait, wait. I knew a guy who said he worked on major league baseball diamonds. He said gasoline was what the big leagues used. You'd dig out a gopher's hole, see. Not too much, just enough to get a rag shoved down. Then about half a cup of gasoline poured on the rag . . ."

"Then light it on fire!"

"No. No. You don't have to light it."

"But that'd be cool."

"Sure, but you don't light the gas in this way of doing it. You just pour it on the rag, then cover up the hole with a little dirt and leave it. Something about the smell of the gas they hate. They just go somewhere else. This guy swore by the gas way. Said they used it all over major league baseball. Everywhere there was a mole or a gopher. He learned it in the minors somewhere, then when he got to the big time, well . . . they already had it there."

I felt my ribs and began to inventory my skeleton for damage.

My sweater and coat must have absorbed some of the kicking that I couldn't remember. I had a sore spot where Christ's disciple had connected. Nothing seemed out of place. My jaw and temple felt raw on the inside as if I'd been the rat in a carnival whack-a-rat. I wondered again out loud what the craziness had been about.

"Accident, the way I see it," another of the regulars who had been a listener up to now. "I think this kind of shit just happens sometimes."

"Oh, that's good. You could make a million on a bumper sticker that says that." This from the gopher-specific guy.

"Very funny. But I mean it. Sometimes a little guy getting back at the world, going off like that, well, it's just an accident who's in the way, when and where it happens. I always think of some little guys as walking time bombs—you'll pardon me Jackson, present company excluded. Who knows what sics 'em on people. And *what* people get sicced upon."

I held the dregs of my beer up to my head. The bartender thought I had hailed another and poured. "So you guess we just walk into stuff like that guy, and there's no way around it. Accidents. I guess. It's just another form of paranoia to not suspect any plot. To suspect there's not any reason behind shit like that."

"I mean, Professor. You'll pardon my saying, but who'd be after a guy like you, a teacher. It's not like you spend your time pissing people off. You're a library guy, am I right? How many enemies can you make in a library?" He paused and ran his tongue over his upper lip. "On the other hand"—and cocked his head at me—"I'm not sure what a professor really does for a living. Are you guys? What do you think he does every day to get a paycheck? He probably teaches a couple of hours a day, talks to students some. But all the rest of the time. . . . It's not like he's framing houses or pumping septic tanks where we pretty much know what a guy's doing all day. A professor must be a pretty good gig, but for the life of me I couldn't tell you how or why."

"You know, he does look a little suspicious, now that you

mention it, Tom. Notice the eyes, how they shift around, never look you straight in the eye or anything. Who knows what kind of secret life a professor lives?"

"Like Batman."

"Yeah, like Batman. Or . . . like the Penguin, maybe. Who knows what kind of master of crime our professor could be. And those guys were sent as a warning, you see. It's all becoming clearer and clearer."

They all broke out laughing. My head in hand, I waved acknowledgment that I was being had, capitulation. I had walked into an accident of time and space. Like Godalming? Like Jane Hunter? How convenient that none of this meant anything. Just the opposite of great texts where everything means. And keeps on meaning and keeps on connecting with other things until the patterns overlap and in the really great ones actually reproduce the way life means. According to tonight, that would make *Hamlet* and *Moby-Dick* meaning just like that little asshole walking in to a bar and taking a dislike to the first person he sees over six foot. Why hadn't I seen this before? "Shit happens," as a literary theory. That ought to be worth a paper, maybe a book. Shit happens in texts and that's how come nobody could figure out the whiteness of the whale. Damn, but this is all going to hurt like hell in the morning. Poor Charlie's had an accident. Everybody has accidents. It's an accidental world we live in. It would be an accident to find in the whole world of oceans the exact white whale that took off your leg. And it would be accidental for that whale then to . . .

I accepted a consolation beer on top of the cold one to hold to my lumped head and the accidentally ordered beer. The guys in the bar had moved on from fate to the subject of probability. How likely is it to pitch a no-hitter? Catch a salmon specially marked with a tag for an ocean salmon derby? One expert remarked that the act of marking the salmon by putting a tag in it would then make it uncatchable for ten days to two weeks while the salmon recovered from the shock of being marked as the $10,000 prize.

Surely the marine biologist knew that and told the people who ran the derby. What was this called, this screwing with the statistical probabilities by interfering with the elements of the problem? Something. It had to have a name because everyone knew that you'd screw up anything natural by submitting it to . . .

"You guys are making my head hurt with this statistics stuff," I said. My head hurt. "A no-hitter is only just possible. That's why it happens once in a while. Because it's possible. Like . . . like what?" An example came to me from Melville's book, *The Confidence-Man*, but I thought better about using it in this crowd. I quoted anyway, "'Hardly anybody believes my story, and so to most I tell a different one.' And that's what happens when someone hits you in the head too many times. And the ribs. And somewhere else that I know I'll be more sure about tomorrow." I laughed at the vacant looks I was getting from the bar guys. Sympathetic but vacant.

"Are you okay? What's the deal about making up stories? Are you okay?"

They all thought that I might need another beer. They all might need another beer. Those jerks weren't coming back. The bar didn't close until two. They listed one after another the certainties of the present. There was a front offshore that would slide north before coming to land. You could tell when the house changed the barrels of draft beer. Each barrel had its own taste. Some were worse than others. Beer tasted better in general if the glass was neither too clean (bleached) nor too cold; those frosty glasses were for tourists in the tourist traps. Women were wonderful in bars but there was a limit, a threshold above which the bar lost its soul and was no longer a good place to drink (instantly declared a mere theory, some dispute here). People who went into politics were by definition the wrong kind of people to be holding office (the corollary of Groucho Marx's assertion that he would never belong to any organization that would have someone like him as a member). The cosmos was unreasonable—or God was cruel, evolution was bitter, the universe was devoid of any meaning—if something that tasted as good as salt turned out to be really bad for you (new basket of pretzels from the bartender). Roasted chicken tasted much better if you poked holes in it while it was still hot to let out the excess oil and if you had drunk at least three beers to soften the impact of the chicken in your stomach. Fishing was really just about getting out of the house.

By the time the conversation had reached God, evolution and the universe, my head had gone from ache to throb. The application of successive beers had done too little by way of anesthesiology. I said out loud what I was thinking.

"I feel like shit. I'm going home." I stood up carefully, using the booth back and the table as crutches.

"Gravity, Professor. Remember the basic rule. Keep the round, the melon part up, and you'll be okay."

"Phases of the moon. Phases of the moon. Never mind that alignment of planets crap. Handle the moon and you'll handle everything." I paused and listened. "That's what I say. I say, 'phases of the moon.'"

* * *

I moved along the sidewalk that dipped regularly to allow for driveways. Each dip meant steady, then down, then back up. I couldn't find the moon or anything moon-like about the night, on shore or off. Down, the concrete undulating. Up, the concrete catching my foot halfway to the ground like climbing stairs. I waited for the night. Out of any shadow might come some of what killed Godalming and Jane. Some flying part of an absent-minded world, some indistinct half-thought of the madly arranged molecules that didn't give a shit about anyone or anything . . . I chuckled to myself and hitched up my pants. That's it, I thought. Just before the apocalypse I'll hitch up my pants. We'll all hitch up our pants.

I paused at a lamppost highly amused at myself. I remembered when I had been crossing a busy street near the hospital and had had an epiphany about my own death. I had been grocery shopping earlier in the day, and as I crossed the busy street where many old people didn't signal their intentions to come around the corner to the hospital, I had a vision of my own demise. One of those blue-haired ladies in a Buick Century would hit me and knock me over without so much as turning her head, eyes intent through the steering wheel, and I would go over pole-axed and my head would split open on the asphalt and a voice would come to me during the splitting and would say, "customer service to the bottle-return please." I had been laughing so hard at this vision that a car making a turn from the other direction nearly got me. "Customer service to the bottle-return please." This would be the last voice from the earthly realm and, I was convinced, would contain all the meaning available on earth. I pictured Godalming in the plastic outhouse reading the white container that held the cake of urinal deodorant when the light failed for him. What was Jane daydreaming about?

The night had split the difference between the ocean and the shore. First the air wafted in my nose, now clearing of bar smoke, of full ocean, mid-Pacific, brilliant molecules of clean spray and salt. The next second the shore drifted over the ocean air like a slow motion return in a ping-pong game. My nose filled with wood smoke, the waft of duff and fir needles and highway oil. Then the ocean came back again. I stood steadying the lamppost against the comings and goings of the two worlds, watery and solid. I thought, "meditation and water are wedded forever" — somewhere from the beginning of *Moby-Dick*. "Spinning, animate and inanimate," from the end of the book. I shrunk down the pole to the ground and sat and said to myself, "at ease, sailor." I laughed since I had amused myself mightily again. I decided I must be sitting down because after trying to walk, I realized I was going nowhere. A light came on above the storefront whose sidewalk I was occupying. The shade went up, and light washed the walk. I wondered how loud I had bid myself at ease. I thought I should stand up. I felt I might like to cry about Jane but couldn't get all the way to the crying place. I felt my head with one hand like fingering a globe looking for an exotic country somewhere . . . somewhere. The lumps felt spongy and irregular. One on my left temple had a small knot in the middle. Knot-head, I thought. The Knot-heads? How did they vote?

On my feet again, out of the window light and off down the street, I felt I was on the verge of deciding, deciding something that wasn't very clear yet, but I *knew* if I chugged along toward home, it would probably become clearer. I inventoried the lumps on my head, and no particular one of those seemed more important than any other one. Tomorrow, I suspected, tomorrow would be another story. The two gentle winds swapped and then swapped again—shore for water, water for shore. As I neared the harbor, a seam of diesel fuel joined the two winds like a bass note shared in each. The fishing boats were black against black water, poking out against the gray-lit sky, poles nearly touching the arc of the bridge. A foghorn. I began to move with more authority as some of the alcohol percolated off, then with more urgency as the beer cleared my kidneys and topped up my bladder. I made it up the stairs to my rooms, past the broken TV, the chair hulking in the dark, the book mess occupying one corner and to the bathroom. "At ease sailor," I said, peeing. "At ease sailor."

So what's the cautionary tale about? I think of Jane and Godalming and my shredded hands. I think of the guy beating on me in the bar. I think I don't know the difference between any of them. If I had them in a story, I could parse the substance, the narrative theory, the patterns and let you know about difference and sameness. That's what I do. What I don't do very well is deal with the whole untidy business of living around real mayhem, bad luck, bad timing. I keep walking into buzz saws not of my own making, and Arvin and his fey treading of the earth like a Celtic spirit popping up from behind natural and unnatural obstacles, his Neolithic take on clouds and wind and sand, Arvin of air, fire and water seems to have pre-known where all this is going—his sister of biblical proportions, his brothers out of a Mickey Spillane novel.

Arvin

Climbing up into the bridge was like finding the best monkey bars ever. The only thing near it I remember was the top of that tree bending and bending and bending until I felt I could clip the ground and clip the sky and watch the ground and then go again. The bridge was dirty to hold on to, but I could see out to the ocean and back up the river like the bending and bending because I climbed through facing out one way and then out the other. That was the easiest way up. I could almost run. In places I didn't need to use hands. The wind was like water. Both of them smelled new and felt new but at the same time made me comfortable.

When I first came to see the professor in Newport, I felt like I wanted to cry almost all the time except when I got up into the bridge, and there it went away. I didn't know why I wanted to cry. I think it was because I didn't want my family anymore: not any one of them with their "poor Arvin," and their "spit it out Arvin," and their "when you're older Arvin." Even when my mothers sighed and put their hands on my head, even then. Climbing the bridge with the papers in my backpack I could have climbed straight off the earth like a rocket to Mars. I felt boosted from below like someone helping me up on the wall, like Carl boosting me up (only he'd do it to knock me off and see how I liked being Humpty Dumpty).

I think the second time up into the bridge was even better in the long run. The pigeons scattered like a bomb was coming, like I was coming, coming to get the papers. The cars above roared. The ocean roared. The pigeons exploded. The sky roared as I came down with the papers in my pack, in my stomach and in my feet. I could run the down-rails and pop to the up-rail of the next one to stop myself. I could hold out my hands to feel the wind off the water and off the sky. I'm going to Mexico with all the money I'll need for everything I want. My family will get the rest and have to like it or lump it. There are seagulls and another big bird I don't know below me. One seems to hang in the air like a kite, not going anywhere as I come down through the X and M shapes of the green iron. A bird is still. There's another and another. I can walk down on them all the way like steps and bring the papers back to earth.

Thorne

The family Kraft could not catch up with Arvin unless he wanted them to, I decided. They returned empty-handed, then I called Gene and I wanted the cavalry too, and Arvin melted somewhere into the infrastructure of Newport: the docks and boats, the tourist traps, the condos stepped up the hill like the devil's infernal ziggurat. Dearly beloved we are gathered here . . . in some kind of commune, some handholding conjunction of disparate parts. This, I thought, is exactly the beautiful messiness of the world I had been avoiding before Arvin.

Salome has not found Arvin and has come to a silent seething. She says to me: "Professor Thorne . . . Professor Thorne . . ." as if she's an engine that can't get going, wheels slipping against the track, engine too powerful and defeated by a lack of traction. Finally she said: "You have become fixed in Arvin's head. We saw it at home after your visit. He ran away to you. He has switched his allegiance from family to you for some unknown reason. His mind is impressionable and fragile in a hard-edged world. He's easy to hurt. You must now be careful around him as we were careful around him when his allegiance was with us." Now she began to pull freight cars. "When he was very little, before he could speak, he was so active that he flew around our house and seemed to vault his little body over everything in its way. It was like nothing so much as flying close to the ground. Neither of the other two boys ever did anything like it. I remember just watching him and thinking that he had a special covenant with gravity, different than anyone else."

I found myself doing what Arvin called "the listen." She bound up the air with the rhythms of her speech. She didn't need to stand on the toes of my shoes to keep me there.

She kept going, encouraged, it seemed, by the sound of her own voice. "Arvin, I will admit, didn't always fascinate me then. My mother became the caregiver. But now Arvin has found his power in our lives, a power he never had in anyone's life before. I'm afraid it might corrupt him absolutely like power can. You, professor, have assumed the role of limits to his power. I believe he will come to you and rely on you. You will be very influential. As a Melville scholar, you certainly have run across similar circumstances in his works. I once read some Melville and recall that he was fascinated by the surfaces of the world."

I was falling into the sound of her and her Melville references. I caught myself and pulled away to watch her fabricate her case for my responsibilities for Arvin. That is, I needed to be out looking for him. He'd reveal himself to me like Hamlet's father's ghost did only to Hamlet. Salome at heart was playful, I decided. Playful in a sort of cunning and con-man way, but playful. She seemed to be needing to connive and felt most comfortable in her conniving mode. I began to think of her as a literary character trying herself out in my life. She stood in my apartment in front of her family (who seemed to become suddenly anaesthetized when she talked, frozen in place as if by some secondary power of her words) and contrived a role for me in the recovery of the lost Arvin. I searched for a response, something short and clever for when she finished. I thought I had it with: "I'll take it under advisement." But no, then occurred to me something biblical: "And what would you like me to do with John the Baptist's head?" Not good either, though it had some panache. Salome didn't admit of panache. Not really of wit either. She seemed as if she might yield to something more blunt-force trauma. Something like: "Up yours, Salome." Or more restrained: "I think the technical term would be, 'in a pig's eye,' Salome." What about the ancient and venerable standard: "Fuck you and the horse you rode in on." I always liked that one. It had folkloric qualities.

I actually said: "Your brother seems to be a complicated person," and let it go at that.

The rest went quickly. Night fell. Arvin did not show up until morning, then knocked on my door, standing there as if he'd just arrived from the East. I fully expected him to give the high sign, recite the password, proffer the shibboleth. Instead he came in, his hooded sweatshirt puffing out his cheeks and giving him the look of Buddha with a head cold.

"Arvin, your family's been looking for you." As it came out of my mouth I saw in his face that I had just explicated the obvious. He said nothing and seemed patient for me to try again. "Arvin," I complied. "Are you okay?" Again I had hit the inane right on the head, and again, Arvin was patient and silent. I figured number three try should have a little class or something more than obvious and inane, so I waited, something I never did in actual conversation; I usually just plunged on. But with Arvin I felt suddenly responsible to actually say something significant. What was it about his hopeful face pulled by the hood into a smush? I found myself giving up the stewardship that Salome had insisted on, the responsibility to hold Arvin in some kind of check. I never had it anyway. It was Salome's capitulation, Salome's negating motherhood and sisterhood at the same time. Salome giving up fried foods and fattening desserts. I thought Salome was missing some circuits. Arvin had the circuits even though they were operating on low voltage.

Finally I said, "Arvin, do you need my help?"

He nodded and said, "I want you to get the papers because you seem to know what to do with them. I want you to have the papers, but be careful because Salome will grab them away. Or Ben. Or Carl. I don't know how to give them to you and get the money and be gone before my family knows I'm gone."

"That's a problem, Arvin. I don't have any money to give you. I have a friend named Gene who says he can get enough money to buy the manuscript but it will take him a few days, maybe even a week or so. I mean I have about $2,000 in my bank account you could have as a down payment. You know how that works? Okay, then I could probably get some more from Gene, maybe $5,000 more. I don't know. That would give you some money to get started in Mexico. And then we could wire you the rest. But the problem doesn't stop there. It's a question of who actually owns the manuscript. Is it yours because you found it? Or does it belong to your whole family? I'm not sure. Are you?"

Arvin loosened his hood and pulled it back. His hair sprouted like a chia pet. After a while he said, "My family is not sure where I got the papers from. I told Salome they were in the house because that's where they were. But they could have been in a box in a hole in the vacant lot near the creek. Then they'd be mine. Buried treasure. I know the rules of buried treasure. She doesn't know if I got them in an antique store or the vacant lot, really. You know what? I don't even think I told her they were in the house anywhere either. Now that would make them completely mine. She doesn't have a very big idea of anything in this case, I think."

"Where are the papers, Arvin? Are they here in Newport?"

"Sorta."

I thought that explicating that "sorta" might take some time. Arvin was a sophist of sorts in his own right. He possessed his own logic and worked effortlessly within it. He was like a live text that made up its own rules and then behaved as if those rules were true.

So "sorta" was going to be it. Arvin, what flitting prerogatives are you keeping from your family, from me, from the world?

Arvin had come to seem familiar to me, not just from seeing him around me in Newport, I think. Something else, and maybe he had brought me the manuscript for the same reason, something else made him seem as if I had known him a much longer time. I entertained the thought, because I had to as a literary person, that what I saw familiar in Arvin was actually the Arvin I knew was in me, in everyone—that damaged but valiant remnant of a god that sucked a deep breath every day and got on with the hard business of living while I couldn't. Get on with the living part, Arvin was teaching me. I know the deaths since the manuscript surfaced had nothing to do with any literary characters, and I also know that any object can become valuable and make regular people into scoundrels and barbarians if it comes to represent enough money. But to Arvin the same pile of papers had meant buying off his sister's wrath, escaping his brothers' tyranny, and finally a surfeit of meatball sandwiches that might represent, what? — some recompense for all he yearned for in life. And Arvin could yearn after. He practiced the yearning.

Arvin

My other mother once saw me run up the side of a house. I could live in the walls like a bug. Salome, even when she was making me do the listen, was always, I think, afraid I would embarrass her and the family before she could make me understand what I was supposed to do.

I come down the inside of the bridge with the papers in my backpack so my hands are free, my feet are free. I can walk through the sky on the birds alone. I can. I don't even need to touch the beams. I run on sunbeams not the green bridge beams with their Ms and Xs. MMMMMMMMMMMMMMM . . . XXXXXXXXXXXXXXXXX. The humming and the wind, the sound of the water saying yes to me. I can walk on the birds below me, tiptoe on the birds all the way down.

Thorne

Carl saw Arvin ascend up into the bridge by laying a driftwood log against the cement pillar, running up it to the top of the pillar and then from there up into the crossbeams of the bridge. Carl went and got Ben, Ben got Salome and his mother. And me. We stood below and watched Arvin scoot into the infrastructure and disappear up under the roadbed. On my first days in Newport, I had walked across the bridge on the sidewalk and about halfway became disoriented and took refuge in a little tower. Once I couldn't see the ocean on one side, the river on the other, the float and tremble of the air beneath me, I could get my wits back, and then I walked the rest of the way across looking down at the walkway instead of out at the air and water.

We all watched Arvin's physical genius, hands and elbows and feet pumping him effortlessly upward until he was gone. We waited without saying a word. Caroline Kraft only wrung her hands and stared up. Salome seemed to pout while she clenched her jaws and ground her teeth slowly. Carl was like a pointer dog onto a bird, quivering with attention. And Ben seemed to be staring up there against his will, seemed to be waiting to be dismissed so he could attend to some other, more important, affair. I stood in the tableau not knowing exactly what my role was. I felt as if I were part of a recording to make sure the world would know what happened there in Newport that day. I thought, I am the witness without whom all of this would be hearsay, family lore and tall tale. The story of Arvin and his family and the manuscript for *Moby-Dick*, the unlikely tale of unlikely characters just like Melville's story. I felt my responsibility deeply and smiled.

The wind had come onshore, and below the traffic noise that resonated on the surface of the bridge, the wind played through the girders like the strings of a guitar. The wind had to work its way through the openings and cross-bracings, seethe along the

175

arches and then out the harbor side. I remember not hearing the wind in the bridge until I had lived with it a couple of years. Listen, a friend told me, and you'll start to hear it. The wind plays the bridge. I found the best time to hear the wind play the bridge was in a medium wind. Strong winds were too noisy and seemed to contain their own engine from the sea. Light winds didn't seem to tickle the strings right. But that day with Arvin having ascended into the interstices of the sky, that swinger of trees Arvin with his song that matched the wind, I stood rocked back on my heels and waited like I had as a child for the bird to come out of my grandfather's cuckoo clock. We looked up into the bridge and waited.

Before long Arvin appeared with his backpack just below the roadway. He paused and looked out toward the ocean and didn't seem to see us. He ran along one girder not using his hands, down another beam and then up a third moving toward the center of the bridge along some pathway that he seemed able to pick out at high speed. There he paused again in a shadow and nearly disappeared into the bridge again. He sat like a bird waiting to fly. Then he scampered off again this time following the contours of an X, then an M. He seemed to be playing rather than trying to come down. Mrs. Kraft had turned away, but Salome, Carl and Ben continued to track Arvin.

Suddenly Arvin bolted down toward a main crossbeam and then seemed to step out into the air with the same motion he used flitting among the steel. He stepped out into the air where gulls and pelicans floated on the wind coming under the bridge. The birds seemed stationary with wings full of gathered air, air that they released slowly then to stay in place. Arvin made stepping motions as if he were walking down the birds to come to earth.

At first he fell slowly, or seemed to, since there was so far to travel between birds, but he picked up speed as we watched him descend bird to bird toward the hard water where he entered with hardly a splash.

"Oh my God," Salome said. "Oh my God."

Arvin's body surfaced almost immediately and was borne landward spread-eagle on the incoming tide. They recovered his body upriver peaceful among the tree roots where the tide ran over the fresh water.

The manuscript for *Moby-Dick* was in the backpack sealed in triple plastic bags and then duct-taped around and around, fit for buried treasure. The impact had shattered it like glass so that the largest fragment was no bigger than dust. He must have fallen directly onto the pack.

Thorne

Gene Anczyski arrived with wire transfers of funds sufficient to buy the manuscript, save the Kraft family and make everything right with the world. But there was no manuscript—a pile of dust, a universal fate. The Kraft family had a thin patch of the manuscript to lay alongside the quart of 19th century dust from Arvin's pack. I thought what they still had might be worth $10,000 as the partial remains of a great American book. Salome mentioned, in her grief, bankruptcy proceedings to delay DaGamma's collections. Jane, I thought, remembering the lines from a favorite author, left an incandescent ring around her burial place. Godalming roiled in the bosom of the earth. And I looked for my trail back to the books where I found my solace. The river came from the land like a song; the ocean slid in under the bridge in regular rhythms and harmonies. And the watery world was everywhere sufficient.

Roundfire

FICTION

Put simply, we publish great stories. Whether it's literary or popular, a gentle tale or a pulsating thriller, the connecting theme in all Roundfire fiction titles is that once you pick them up you won't want to put them down.
If you have enjoyed this book, why not tell other readers by posting a review on your preferred book site. Recent bestsellers from Roundfire are:

The Bookseller's Sonnets
Andi Rosenthal

The Bookseller's Sonnets intertwines three love stories with a tale of religious identity and mystery spanning five hundred years and three countries.
Paperback: 978-1-84694-342-3 ebook: 978-184694-626-4

Birds of the Nile
An Egyptian Adventure
N.E. David

Ex-diplomat Michael Blake wanted a quiet birding trip up the Nile – he wasn't expecting a revolution.
Paperback: 978-1-78279-158-4 ebook: 978-1-78279-157-7

Blood Profit$
The Lithium Conspiracy
J. Victor Tomaszek, James N. Patrick, Sr.

The blood of the many for the profits of the few... Blood Profit$
will take you into the cigar-smoke-filled room where American
policy and laws are really made.
Paperback: 978-1-78279-483-7 ebook: 978-1-78279-277-2

The Burden
A Family Saga
N.E. David

Frank will do anything to keep his mother and father apart. But
he's carrying baggage – and it might just weigh him down ...
Paperback: 978-1-78279-936-8 ebook: 978-1-78279-937-5

The Cause
Roderick Vincent

The second American Revolution will be a fire lit from an
internal spark.
Paperback: 978-1-78279-763-0 ebook: 978-1-78279-762-3

Don't Drink and Fly
The Story of Bernice O'Hanlon: Part One
Cathie Devitt

Bernice is a witch living in Glasgow. She loses her way in her
life and wanders off the beaten track looking for the garden of
enlightenment.
Paperback: 978-1-78279-016-7 ebook: 978-1-78279-015-0

Gag
Melissa Unger

One rainy afternoon in a Brooklyn diner, Peter Howland punctures
an egg with his fork. Repulsed, Peter pushes the plate away and
never eats again.
Paperback: 978-1-78279-564-3 ebook: 978-1-78279-563-6

The Master Yeshua
The Undiscovered Gospel of Joseph
Joyce Luck

Jesus is not who you think he is. The year is 75 CE. Joseph ben Jude
is frail and ailing, but he has a prophecy to fulfil ...
Paperback: 978-1-78279-974-0 ebook: 978-1-78279-975-7

On the Far Side, There's a Boy
Paula Coston

Martine Haslett, a thirty-something 1980s woman, plays hard on
the fringes of the London drag club scene until one night which
prompts her to sign up to a charity. She writes to a young Sri Lan-
kan boy, with consequences far and long.
Paperback: 978-1-78279-574-2 ebook: 978-1-78279-573-5

Tuareg
Alberto Vazquez-Figueroa

With over 5 million copies sold worldwide, *Tuareg*
is a classic adventure story from best-selling author Alberto
Vazquez-Figueroa, about honour, revenge and a clash of cultures.
Paperback: 978-1-84694-192-4

Readers of ebooks can buy or view any of these bestsellers by clicking on the live link in the title. Most titles are published in paperback and as an ebook. Paperbacks are available in traditional bookshops. Both print and ebook formats are available online.

Find more titles and sign up to our readers' newsletter at
http://www.johnhuntpublishing.com/fiction

Follow us on Facebook at https://www.facebook.com/JHPfiction
and Twitter at https://twitter.com/JHPFiction

For more than forty years,
Yearling has been the leading name
in classic and award-winning literature
for young readers.

Yearling books feature children's
favorite authors and characters,
providing dynamic stories of adventure,
humor, history, mystery, and fantasy.

Trust Yearling paperbacks to entertain,
inspire, and promote the love of reading
in all children.

OTHER YEARLING BOOKS YOU WILL ENJOY